WRITTEN IN THE STARS

When Sophie Blaze's hopes of becoming a policewoman are dashed, she does the next best thing and becomes a private enquiry agent. Jogging in the park, she bumps into her old school friend, Emma Mountjoy, who asks her to investigate a family mystery. Sophie has no idea that her enquiries will lead her to handsome widower Jack West. But from their very first meeting they clash when Jack mistakes Sophie for an investigative journalist intent on getting a scoop.

MARGARET MOUNSDON

WRITTEN IN THE STARS

Complete and Unabridged

LINFORD
Leicester

First published in Great Britain in 2011

First Linford Edition
published 2012

British Library CIP Data

Mounsdon, Margaret.
    Written in the stars. - -
(Linford romance library)
1. Love stories.
2. Large type books.
I. Title II. Series
823.9′2–dc23

ISBN 978–1–4448–1110–0

Published by
F. A. Thorpe (Publishing)
Anstey, Leicestershire

Set by Words & Graphics Ltd.
Anstey, Leicestershire
Printed and bound in Great Britain by
T. J. International Ltd., Padstow, Cornwall

This book is printed on acid-free paper

Meeting An Old Acquaintance

'Bryony, heel!' Sophie bellowed. The over-excited dog took no notice of her command and barked happily at the skittish piebald, her pink tongue lolling in anticipation of a game.

The horse rolled its eyes, stalled and did its best to unseat its elegant rider.

'Get away, you stupid mutt.' She tightened her reins and dug her knees into the piebald's flanks. 'Can't you control your dog?' the rider shouted at Sophie.

'Sorry.' Sophie managed to catch hold of Bryony's collar and drag her away. 'She doesn't mean any harm. She only wants to play.'

Bryony's tail thumped Sophie's legs as her sturdy body strained against her mistress's hold.

'We were out for a jog,' Sophie

1

gasped, 'and she always gets excited when we run.'

By now her blonde hair had worked its way free from its scrunchie. She tried to flick her fringe out of her eyes aware she was more than overdue for a visit to the hairdresser. She knew she made a scruffy contrast to the young woman still trying to take charge of her mount.

'Are you sure you're fit to own a dog?'

The tone of the horse rider's voice sent Bryony off into a new fever of barking and the piebald seized that moment to rear. Caught unawares, the rider slid gracefully off her mount and landed in the mud. With a whinny of success and toss of its head, the piebald, at last free of its burden, cantered off.

Aghast, Sophie could only stare at the upended sight of two jodhpur-clad legs flailing in the air.

'Are you all right?' she asked.

'No, I'm not,' came the outraged reply.

From the tone of her voice Sophie realised with relief that the only thing the rider seemed to have hurt was her dignity.

'Help me up,' she commanded.

Privately feeling the rider deserved a soaking for suggesting that her dog didn't know how to behave in the park, Sophie was only sorry she hadn't been ditched in a bigger pool of muddy water.

'Sorry,' she fibbed, secretly wanting to congratulate the horse. 'Got to hold on to Bryony. You'll have to get yourself up.'

She watched the shapely legs continue to flail like windmill sails. Eventually the rider righted herself and struggled to maintain a more dignified position.

'If any harm's come to my horse, I'll sue you.' She grabbed up her fallen riding hat and ramming it back on her head glared at Sophie.

'The park is common land,' Sophie pointed out. 'I've every right to be here

3

and you did thunder at us out of nowhere. It's no wonder Bryony was spooked.'

'Where's Beauty?' Sophie's robust protest was ignored.

A gentle whinny reassured Sophie that the horse had suffered no injury.

'Look,' she tried to make amends, 'there's no need to fall out about this. I know Bryony barked at Beauty, but it won't happen again. I promise.'

'It had better not.'

'I'm Sophie Blaze,' Sophie introduced herself with a sigh. Conciliation was clearly not an option. The situation looked as though it could turn nasty. 'I'd better know your name?'

'Emma Mountjoy,' was the reluctant reply.

She thrust Sophie's business card into her pocket without glancing at it then strode towards Beauty who was still happily cropping grass.

Sophie clipped a lead on to Bryony's collar. The trusting eyes, now suspiciously docile, looked up into hers. If

dogs could wink then Bryony was definitely guilty of surreptitiously closing
one eyelid in a conspiracy of amusement. Sophie crammed her hair back
into her baseball cap and tried to repair
the damage to her mud-spattered leg-
gings.

'You are a naughty girl,' Sophie
chided Bryony who merely wagged her
tail in response. 'Now, no more trouble,
do you hear?'

Finished with her hair and giving up
on the mud, Sophie looked back to
where Emma was still fussing round her
horse.

'Don't I know you?' she enquired
politely.

The question met with a wall of
silence. With her back turned to Sophie,
Emma carried on inspecting her horse's
fetlocks for injury. As the silence grew
embarrassing Sophie shrugged, turned
away and began jogging back towards
the footpath.

'Come on, Bry, but take it easy,' she
urged. 'Remember park etiquette. Other

people need to use the facilities.'

Keeping fit was not one of Sophie's passions but in her job it was a necessity. It was no good trying to keep pace with her quarry if she was in danger of falling at the first fence, not that much chasing after miscreants had been required so far. All the same it was as well to be prepared. Sophie knew if you felt fit in your body, you were fit in your mind.

She began to breathe more heavily and the muscles in her legs strained under the increased pressure as she pounded along.

Emma Mountjoy. At first Sophie hadn't recognised her. It had been a few years since they'd seen each other, but as Emma scrambled around in the long grass looking for her riding hat there had been no mistaking the haughty expression in those piercing amber eyes or the clipped tone of her voice.

How could Sophie forget the school sports captain? For a while Emma had been the bane of Sophie's life. Like all her set, Emma Mountjoy was a bit of a bully, and less privileged girls such as Sophie didn't stand a chance against her. Many was the wet winter afternoon Sophie had been forced to run around a muddy football pitch, fighting for breath, wearing nothing more than a thin T shirt and shorts, all because she'd tried to shy off games.

'Best thing for a cold is a dose of fresh air.' Emma would rout Sophie out of the comfort of the snug warmth of the classroom and force her into her sports clothes. 'Now get running.'

In those days Sophie may have been a bit of a wimp when it came to sports, but she wasn't a tell tale. She could have gone to the head teacher and reported Emma for her bullying, but Sophie had more pride than to give in to someone like Emma Mountjoy. With gritted teeth she always completed the course and eventually a reluctant respect had grown up between the two girls. After a while Emma had left her alone and Sophie had been surprised to find that while she still never really enjoyed jogging, it wasn't such a penance any more.

After she'd left school and gone to college, Sophie had not seen Emma Mountjoy again — until today.

Sophie thought the years had treated her kindly. She looked tanned and confident. Her russet hair was no longer tied in a wiry plait. It was fixed back in a neat pleat, expensively styled and highlighted.

She was far happier when Bryony forced her out on to the common for a five-mile jog. It was only occasionally they missed a day — like yesterday when the weather had been too wet to jog, and that was why Bryony had barked at Beauty. It had been nothing more than high spirits, but Sophie hadn't been given the chance to explain to Emma. The years may have passed but she still looked in no mood to listen to anything Sophie had to say.

Sophie and Bryony reached the edge

of the lake and Sophie glanced over her shoulder. There was no sign of Emma or Beauty. Hopefully Emma wouldn't carry through her threat to prosecute Sophie. From the way she strode towards her horse, it didn't look as though she had broken any bones and the animal wasn't injured either.

Sophie took a few moments out to catch her breath. The April air was fresh with the promise of spring. It had been a cold night, frosty in parts, but now the sun was gaining in strength and the park sparkled.

Sophie looked down at the sludge-coloured blades of grass peeping through the frost. Grass was never brilliant green to her. Nor were roses ever bright red. The most she could manage was a pale pink and a sludgy shade of green.

It had been the biggest disappointment of Sophie's life to be turned down for the police force. Her condition was not serious, but enough to cut her aspirations short. Not all colours were confusing to her, but the ones that mattered — red and green, were too important for her to be considered a suitable applicant. The day she had failed the medical had been the biggest disappointment of her life. Ever since she'd been a child, it had been her ambition to follow in her father's footsteps.

Her mother, on the other hand, had been relieved that her daughter was not going to follow family tradition.

'You don't know how I used to worry about your father,' she confided to Sophie. 'Every time he was late home, or involved in a special operation my imagination went into overdrive. I know how disappointed you must be, darling, but I don't think I could stand it if anything happened to you in the course of your duty.'

Until then Sophie had no idea her eyesight was flawed. She wasn't sure where the idea of being a private enquiry agent came from, but now a few months after setting up her agency,

Sophie realised she had made the right choice.

Several of her contemporaries had fallen out of love with the idea of pounding the beat, or filling in countless forms. Sophie, on the other hand, loved her new life.

The pleasure when she reunited an owner with a lost pet or traced a missing relative was worth more than a king's ransom, and for a small market town, Steepways provided a surprisingly brisk turnover of work.

Set deep in the North Downs, Sophie had expected business to be on the quiet side, but her clientele, sometimes seeking anonymity, were prepared to travel from outside the area to consult her. Her father, now retired, had provided an invaluable source of local contacts, and occasionally helped out on some of her cases.

As Sophie watched the powerboats skimming across the lake, she became aware of the thud of hooves behind her.

'Bryony, heel,' she called out quickly,

biting down her exasperation.

Bryony bounded back to her and Sophie re-clipped the lead to her collar. It looked as though Emma Mountjoy, now she had recovered her dignity, was going to take things further.

'Sophie Blaze? It is you, isn't it?'

'Yes, it's me, Emma,' she said calmly.

These days Sophie had seen far too much of life to let the likes of Emma Mountjoy intimidate her. If Emma wanted a showdown then Sophie wasn't about to roll over and surrender like she had done in the past.

'Are you really a private enquiry agent?' A puzzled frown creased Emma's smooth brow as she waved Sophie's business card at her. It was as if she still couldn't quite place her.

'I am.'

There was a creak of leather as Emma eased her position in her saddle.

'What do you do for a living?' Sophie felt emboldened to ask.

'Me?' Emma looked surprised by the question. 'I'm an artist, actually.'

It was Sophie's turn to raise her eyebrows.

'You mean you paint for a living?'

A reluctant smile softened Emma's rosebud lips. 'Is it any more peculiar than being a snoop?'

'Not really, no,' Sophie conceded. 'I suppose I never imagined you having a job.'

'You have to go where the money is,' Emma confided.

'I thought,' Sophie hesitated, aware that what she had been about to say sounded rather rude, 'that, well, living where you do . . . ' she let the rest of her statement trail.

'Lived,' Emma corrected her.

'You mean you don't occupy the Manor House any more?'

Emma shook her head. 'Daddy died and all that was left was enough for me to get myself a studio and a small allowance.'

Sophie was at a loss to know what to say. A studio and an allowance of any sort didn't sound too much like hardship to her.

'Look,' Emma hesitated, 'do you think we could meet up some time?'

'You mean for a meal or something?' Sophie asked. Until that moment she had been expecting to be asked the name of her solicitor.

Emma looked confused by the suggestion. 'No.' She shook her head. 'I was thinking you might be able to help me out with a business proposition, actually. There's something I'd like you to do for me.'

'Ah, of course.' A rueful smile hovered on Sophie's lips. The likes of Emma Mountjoy did not socialise with the Sophie Blazes of this world.

'I would value your advice and I don't know where else to go.'

'I'm intrigued,' Sophie said, noticing that Emma really did look worried. 'What's it all about?'

'Something rather strange has happened to me, actually.'

'I'd be more than pleased to help out, if I can,' Sophie offered.

The expression on Emma's face was one Sophie recognised because she'd seen it many times before. It was the expression of someone who was in trouble and they didn't know what to do about it.

'I mean, are you discreet?' Emma leaned forward. 'Can I rely on you to keep things confidential? I wouldn't want anybody finding out.'

'Coming from you I wouldn't have thought that question was necessary,' Sophie reminded her quietly.

It was a vague reference to Emma's past behaviour towards Sophie and from the flush that now stained Emma's elegant neck, Sophie knew her barb had hit home. It would only have taken one word from Sophie to the head teacher for Emma to be in serious trouble for the treatment she had meted out to Sophie.

'Sorry,' Emma apologised, 'my remark was out of order.'

Sophie never one to bear a grudge, nodded in acknowledgement. 'That's all right.'

'Look.' Emma glanced over her shoulder as if she were fearful they might be overheard. 'We can't talk here. Are you free tonight?'

'Yes,' Sophie admitted.

'Can you come to my studio about eight?'

'If you like.'

'I'll tell you all about it then. See you later.'

She turned her horse around and rode off before Sophie had a chance to ask her the whereabouts of her studio.

'What do we do, Bry?'

The dog barked.

'You're right. We're not in a position to turn down what could be a lucrative job. Let's go home. If I can't find out where Emma Mountjoy's studio is located, then I'm not the detective I thought I was.'

'Can You Find Out What Happened?'

Sophie always wore a charcoal grey trouser suit for first meetings with clients. She also fixed her long hair into a top-knot to keep recalcitrant curls off her face. Make-up too she kept to a minimum, just some mascara and a dash of lip-gloss.

Tonight she decided to lessen the formality of her appearance with a fluorescent pink T shirt portraying a rock concert slogan. Emma, she suspected would appreciate the gesture. Too stuffy an image would possibly restrict her confidences, and in Sophie's experience there always were little details that needed to be coaxed from clients. She needed Emma to feel relaxed in her company.

A quick trawl of Emma's details on

the computer revealed the extent of her qualifications. To Sophie's surprise Emma had been modest about her career achievements. Her reputation was highly regarded in artistic circles and several examples of her work had been hung in prestigious galleries. Her particular areas of expertise were scenes from country life, most of them with an equine influence.

To her shame, Sophie had suspected Emma of no more than playing with the idea of being an artist, before settling down with a suitable husband and producing two beautiful, talented children, who like their mother would ride and mix with the right friends.

All of which made their chance encounter that afternoon more perplexing. Sophie had learned from her background research on Emma that her father, Sir Gerald, had died the previous summer. She remembered that Emma was an only child. There had been no mention of her mother. Sophie couldn't recall if she had ever seen either of Emma's parents at school open days but if they had been there, she very much doubted they would have mixed with her parents.

Sophie's fees had been funded by a scholarship and as such Sophie had been expected to work hard and achieve good grades, something Emma and her friends did not appreciate or understand. Whilst they didn't exactly disrupt classes the idea of swotting for an exam was not for them. They played tennis, swam and competed in the school sports, winning cups and trophies that were prominently displayed in the main hall.

In all her years at school, Sophie never won a trophy of any sort.

She decided to walk to her appointment with Emma, whose studio she had discovered was situated in the Stable Yard, an industrial unit on the outskirts of Steepways, an area Sophie knew fairly well. She suspected Emma was a fairly new arrival as in the course of her work, Sophie had had occasion to visit the Stable Yard several times and had never bumped into her.

The industrial unit was prettier than its description implied. Situated down a leafy country lane, the reception area was housed in an old cottage that had once been part of a landed estate.

Ducks circled the pond in the garden and free-range hens scratched around in the grass. Daffodils graced a grassy bank by the little hut at the gate. It was a charming scene and always lifted Sophie's spirits. She waved to the guard on duty, recognising him as one of the regulars.

'I've come to visit Emma Mountjoy, Bill,' she called over.

'I'll sign you in,' he called back. 'Number 6A, follow the path round to the left. You can't miss it.'

Metallic noises in the background indicated that someone was at work on a piece of machinery and Sophie could hear a radio playing classical piano music. The units were of solid construction, sturdily built, most of them with large windows that let in natural light, ideal conditions for an artist. Attempts to personalise their frontage were evident from the selection of posters and tubs of orange geraniums outside. One even sported an old-fashioned petrol pump.

Patting her shoulder bag, which contained her digital camera, tape recorder and notebooks, Sophie reached Emma's unit and rang the bell.

'Come on up,' Emma's voice crackled through the loudspeaker at the door.

The mezzanine room was surprisingly airy and state of the art. The floors were covered with brightly covered throws and Emma had decorated the studio with a few photos and vases of butter yellow chrysanthemums. Sophie wrinkled her nose trying to identify the smell pervading the atmosphere.

'It's lavender polish, one of the scents that help to create a good impression.' Emma was now wearing a casual fluffy sweater and pale blue cargo pants. 'Actually I just squirt an aerosol about the place and hope for the best. It was a trick I learned at art school. It encourages people to linger, and if they linger they might buy something.'

Now she wasn't glaring down at Sophie from astride her horse, the two girls were more or less of an equal height.

'Where do you stable your horse?' Sophie asked.

'Beauty?' Emma looked amused by the question. 'She's not mine.'

'She's not?'

'No, she belongs to a friend. I exercise her occasionally. It helps keep us both in trim. That's why I was so worried about her when I thought your dog might have caused an injury.'

'I'm sorry,' Sophie apologised, 'I didn't realise.'

'It was as much my fault as yours, I suppose,' Emma admitted. 'I was thinking about other things and didn't see Bryony until it was too late. Anyway, you didn't come here to talk about lavender polish and dogs; did you? Sit down.'

Emma indicated a squashy sofa. 'Do

you often work late?' Sophie eyed the camp bed in the corner.

'I'm not really supposed to stay overnight but Bill, he's one of the guards . . . '

'I know him.'

'He turns a blind eye. Equine paintings help pay the bills and some of my more regular clients are quite demanding so I need to put in the hours.'

'I've been researching your career,' Sophie replied. 'I had no idea you were so highly regarded.'

Emma arched a plucked eyebrow. 'I don't only play tennis and swim.'

'No, sorry. I wasn't suggesting you did.'

'What did you do after we left school?'

'I went to college and tried for the police force, but I failed the medical.'

'That's hard.' Emma sounded sympathetic.

'Did you go to art school?'

'For a while, but I prefer to do my own thing. I ducked out after my father died and like you I decided to set up on my own.'

'And when you're not sleeping over, where do you live now?' Sophie asked.

'I have a room in a friend's house. She runs a livery stable and Beauty is her horse. I help out occasionally, taking children for riding lessons, that sort of thing.'

Sophie began to suspect she might have seriously misjudged Emma. To her trained eye it looked as though the girl may have fallen on hard times. She began to feel a pang of compassion for her reduced circumstances and a reluctant admiration for the way she had turned her talents to painting.

'The trouble is my friend also has a young family,' Emma grimaced, 'and a husband and sometimes, well, they're going through a difficult patch and it's better to stay out of everyone's way.'

With her enviably slim figure and striking red hair, Sophie could understand what Emma was saying. Her presence could possibly inflame an already tense family situation.

'Would you like a drink?' Emma

offered. 'I've some herbal tea.'

'Tea will be fine.' Sophie put down her bag and picked a stray hair off the collar of her jacket.

'You look very efficient,' Emma commented as she plugged in the kettle.

Sophie draped her jacket over the back of the sofa, revealing the boy band slogan on her tee shirt.

'I spoke too soon,' Emma laughed at the slogan. 'What's with that?'

'They're very good.'

'I'll take your word for it.' Emma stirred the tea.

'Are you into heavy metal?'

'The classics are more my scene.'

She offered Sophie one of the mugs.

'I suppose we should get down to business,' Sophie began. She produced her mini recorder. 'Do you mind?'

A shadow crossed Emma's face.

'Is it absolutely necessary?' she asked.

'No, but it helps me to make an accurate record of what is said. Of course, I won't use it if you prefer me not to.'

'No.' Emma shook her head. 'As long as everything that passes between us is confidential?'

'I work alone. I do occasionally ask my father to help in my investigations.'

'He was a policeman, wasn't he?' Emma sipped at her tea.

'Yes, but he's retired now. He knows where to go for information, things like that, but I can assure you he's one hundred percent discreet. I never divulge the names of my clients if I have to use him for any background work, so he would have no idea who you were or what the case was about.'

'Am I a case?' A dimple dented Emma's cheek.

'Let's see, shall we? You may not think I'm suited to the task in hand.' Sophie flicked down her Biro and opened her notepad. 'Now what's the problem?'

'I hardly know where to start,' Emma admitted.

'Is it something to do with your father?' Sophie suggested.

'Sort of. You see, he died last summer. My mother is still alive, but she and Daddy divorced years ago when I was a baby. She married again and moved abroad. I don't see her very often. I stayed here with my father and my aunt and uncle. They didn't have a family of their own so my aunt sort of became my mother.'

Sophie was careful not to let her surprise show. Coming from a close-knit family unit, she could never understand how families lost touch with each other. The thought of not seeing her mother regularly filled her with sadness.

'My mother and I exchange cards at Christmas and birthdays but,' Emma frowned, 'Australia's a long way off and the fare is very expensive.'

'So after your father died you had to move house?' Sophie felt a twinge of sympathy for Emma and decided to move the conversation on.

'It was never Daddy's house. My uncle, his brother, owned it. I would have been able to carry on living there, but at the beginning of the year my uncle died as well and his widow, my aunt, wanted to sell up and move. Of course it was a tremendous shock, but I understood her reasons. It took ages to sort everything out. Twenty-eight years in one house is a long time. I sold what I could then stored the remainder of my father's things. Last week I had some spare time on my hands and I started to go through his personal papers. It was something I should have done before, but I just never got round to it.'

Emma stood up and went over to a desk. She extracted a large buff envelope from a drawer and handed it over.

'I found this.'

She tipped the contents on to the coffee table. Inside was another smaller envelope. It contained a lock of baby's hair. Sophie picked it up and examined it, then turned over the envelope. There was no date or details on the outside.

'Yours?' she asked Emma. The colour of the hair was a faded shade of gold.

'I don't think so.' Emma passed over some newspaper cuttings. 'These were also in the envelope.'

The clippings smelt musty as if they had lain undisturbed for a long time. Sophie unfolded them carefully.

'Who are Tony and Naomi Baxter?' she asked as she finished reading the article about them.

'I have absolutely no idea,' Emma replied. 'And neither can I see why my father should keep a newspaper cutting about their disappearance.'

'Have you tried asking your aunt?'

'She's gone to live with an old school friend in Italy and quite frankly she's had enough to worry about this last year. I don't want to stir up a hornet's nest.'

Sophie nodded. 'I see. What would you like me to do about it?' she asked refolding the clippings and putting them back in the envelope.

'Can you find out what happened?' Emma leaned forward, her amber eyes earnest, as if the matter was of tremendous importance to her.

'Surely it was all gone into at the time? I mean people, a whole family, doesn't just disappear leaving no trace?'

'I've tried tracking them on the Internet but it seems that's exactly what happened. One day they were there, the next day they were gone. At first it was thought something gruesome might have happened, but no bodies were ever found. The whole thing is a complete mystery.'

'And you don't know of any connection your father had with the family?'

'No, and I don't really have time to go looking for them.'

'Reading through these reports, it doesn't look as though Tony and Naomi Baxter broke the law.'

'I know there's very little to go on, but can you help?' Emma asked.

'I can try,' Sophie said slowly, 'but can you tell me why you are so interested in the case after all this time?'

Emma blinked her eyelashes several times. Sophie sensed that for some reason she was nervous.

'No, I can't,' Emma replied after a minimal pause.

'Is there any particular reason why you can't?'

'I,' Emma hesitated again, 'no.' She shook her head. 'You don't need to know, do you?'

'It would help my enquiry,' Sophie said, 'but if you don't want to tell me then that is your right.'

'But this is the sort of thing you do?'

'I'm an enquiry agent, so I'll do anything legal within reason.'

'We haven't discussed fees,' Emma said.

'I have a flat daily rate plus expenses.' Sophie was prepared for this question and slid a sheet of paper across the coffee table.

Emma picked it up. 'You're not cheap.' She raised her eyebrows.

Sophie recapped her pen. 'Like you, I have to earn my living. If you'd like to think about it,' she said, 'you have my number.'

'I, er,' Emma looked thoughtful. 'I suppose I could always add a little extra on to my latest equine commission. Framing costs can be expensive.'

'You could try another agency, if you prefer. Rates do vary.'

'No.' Emma pondered her decision, 'If I'm going to go through with this I prefer to deal with someone I know.'

Sophie picked up her recorder and began to repack her bag. In her experience prospective clients often liked a day or two to think about things. Emma, she suspected, would not contact her again. It had been interesting seeing her old school friend, but she doubted their paths would cross much in the future.

'I'll go for it.' Emma nodded and produced her chequebook.

'You don't have to pay me now,' Sophie insisted, taken by surprise by the suddenness of her acceptance.

'I'd better. I may change my mind in the morning.' Emma tore the cheque out and blew on her vivid purple ink to dry it. 'I'll pay you a month's flat fee and you can let me have a list of your expenses later. How's that?'

'More than generous,' Sophie agreed.

Now the business of the day was done, Emma looked keen to finish their interview.

'How would you like to keep in touch?' Sophie asked. 'I could email updates to you on a daily basis?'

Emma shook her head. 'I'd rather you came here personally. Emails aren't all that confidential are they?'

'If you insist,' Sophie replied wondering why Emma was so touchy about computer contact.

'When I'm not around Jack West takes my messages. We're old friends. He runs the garage and re-spray centre opposite in unit 6B. If he's around now introduce yourself to him.'

Outside again in the fresh air, Sophie took a moment to check over Jack's unit. It had a double frontage and there was evidence of recent activity but it looked closed up for the day. Puddles of muddy oil stained water created pools of rainbow colour and a smell of paint lingered on the air.

Sophie wondered if Jack West and Emma were an item. She wore no rings, but Sophie suspected Emma was the sort of girl who would feel incomplete without a man.

'Hello.'

A voice behind her made her jump. She turned and came face to face with a man in a boiler suit.

'Jack West.' He introduced himself. 'And you are?'

'Sophie Blaze.'

He nodded at her T shirt slogan. 'Are they any good?' he asked, referring to the band.

'I think so,' she replied, immediately warming to his friendly smile.

He had oily fingers, she noticed. She liked men who got their hands dirty when they worked. Years ago her father had done up an old car in his spare time and they had spent many happy hours together in his garage sanding

parts down and fitting new compo-
nents.

'Can I do anything for you?' he
enquired.

'What?' Sophie drew her thoughts
back to the present. 'Oh, yes. I'm here
because of Emma Mountjoy. I'm
making enquiries . . . '

'If you're the press,' his smile was
replaced with a quick frown, 'I've got
nothing to say.'

'The press?' Sophie repeated in
confusion.

Jack caught sight of her tape recorder
in her shoulder bag. 'You can put that
thing away, too, and if I ever catch you
round here again pestering Miss Mountjoy there'll be trouble.'

'No, you don't understand,' Sophie
attempted to detain him by putting a
hand on his arm. He shook her off.

'Excuse me. I'm busy. Some of us
have respectable work to do.'

He left Sophie gaping outside his unit
as he strode away from her. If this was
the Jack West who was supposed to be

so helpful, then they had clearly got off to a bad start.

Obviously Jack knew something about Emma that Sophie didn't. What other reason could there be for him to accuse her of snooping? And why on earth should he think she was a reporter?

The hairs on the back of Sophie's neck tingled as her Irish grandmother's sixth sense kicked in. Something was telling her there was more to this case than met the eye.

The Investigation Begins

Sophie parked her hatchback on the village green under the shade of a spreading elm tree. The drive from Steepways had taken little more than half an hour. She had hoped Berkham would be more of a market town, but a quick survey revealed it comprised no more than a convenience store and a Norman church all situated around a square of green in the middle of which stood a war memorial commemorating those who lost their lives in the conflict.

'Come on, Bryony,' Sophie said, making sure the lead was clipped to her collar. They hadn't had their daily jog and, as Berkham looked a horsey sort of place, she didn't want any repeat of last week's incident with Emma Mountjoy.

It was a lazy time of day, early afternoon, and Sophie had timed her visit with care. At this hour most people would be out at work. What she was hoping for was perhaps to find a retired couple with time on their hands, or someone doing a spot of gardening. They were often the type of people who welcomed the chance to chat.

Sophie tried to gather her thoughts as she wondered if anyone living in Berkham would remember Tony and Naomi Baxter. Twenty years was a long time. Even if they did remember the incident, would they be prepared to talk to her? It was a situation that would require a high degree of tact and diplomacy.

The disappearance must have caused quite a stir at the time but it was history and people had short memories. Sophie didn't hold out much hope for a result.

Sophie's sketchy online enquiries had revealed that the Baxters kept themselves to themselves. Neither of them had close family so their disappearance was not immediately reported. A sharp-eyed postman noticed mail hanging out of the letterbox one day and suspicions were aroused. No-one could recall when Naomi or Tony had last been seen around the village. The media lapped up the story, but with no fresh developments, interest eventually waned and other stories took over the headlines. Apart from the occasional inaccurate report that the family had been spotted in a supermarket or on a service station forecourt, nothing further was heard of them.

It was an intriguing case. Sophie was as mystified as the police had been at the time.

Bryony barked happily in the grass as she circled the memorial searching out fresh delights. A dog was always a good companion on occasions like this. Sophie was pleased she had brought her along. Bryony often helped to break the ice. People felt reassured by the presence of a friendly animal and were more forthcoming with their confidences.

For her part, Sophie had taken great pains with her appearance. The older generation usually responded well to a modern girl in her twenties, if she looked attractive, so she had chosen a yellow blouse and matched it with a short floral skirt. Her hair she had deliberately left a little untidy. Too co-ordinated an appearance could created a professional image and arouse suspicion. More than once Sophie had been mistaken for a reporter and doors had been closed in her face, which was always an unpleasant experience.

The memory of her recent encounter with Jack West still smarted. Sophie's generous mouth tightened. She would enjoy putting him in his place. Again Sophie wondered briefly why the press should be interested in Emma. Was that the reason she had employed Sophie to look into this past mystery? Was a big news story about to break?

Sophie had her background story well prepared. She would explain that an old friend had found some press cuttings amongst her father's personal effects. In Sophie's experience it was always as well to keep as near as possible to the truth. Emma was an old friend and she had discovered the newspaper in her father's desk so that part of Sophie's story was true.

This old friend, Sophie decided, was very upset to learn that her father's friends had seemingly disappeared and had asked Sophie to see if she could find out what had happened to the Baxters. If pressed Sophie would exercise her imagination about the two families originally having lost touch due to house moves or something like that. The story was vague on detail but held enough of the ring of truth to be convincing.

The little row of terraced cottages where the Baxters used to live was situated in Church Street at the bottom of the village, away from the memorial. Sophie was pleased to find the area was still unspoiled. So much of the countryside had come up for development and what was a forecourt and garage one day would often be a block of flats within the month.

Careful to leave her tape recorder and camera in the boot of her car, Sophie picked up her bag, locked the door and made for cottage number three.

'Come on, Bryony.' She tugged at the lead. 'Time to go to work.'

She rang the bell. In the distance a dog began to bark.

'Quiet,' an unfriendly voice bellowed.

Through the frosted glass Sophie saw a shape making its way down the hall.

'Yes?'

The man who answered the door glowered at her. The animal he was restraining looked more of a guard dog than a domestic pet. In the background Sophie could hear a television going full blast.

'Keep your dog under control,' he commanded Sophie as the two animals eyed each other up.

Sensing a threat to her mistress, Bryony emitted a low growl.

'Good morning,' Sophie began with

her politest smile.

'Whatever it is you're selling, we're not interested.'

The door was closed in her face before she could get any further. Bryony trembled beside her mistress. Sophie felt pretty much like trembling herself. She patted Bryony's sturdy hindquarters in a gesture of reassurance.

'Let's try next door.'

Now the threat of attack had receded, Bryony trotted happily along to the next cottage. Despite repeated knocking there was no response.

'Doesn't look like our lucky day, does it?' Sophie sighed down at Bryony. 'We could try the local shop, I suppose.'

'Excuse me,' a female voice interrupted her.

Sophie glanced up. A white-haired woman carrying a shopping basket was walking towards her.

'Hello.' Sophie smiled at her, pleased at last to encounter a friendly face.

'Can I help you?'

'Yes, I . . . '

'You want to avoid those people in number three,' she confided. 'Unless they're friends of yours, of course?'

'No, they're not,' Sophie insisted.

'They get up to some very odd things, callers all hours of the day and night.'

'I see.' Sophie angled her body language to invite further confidence.

'Yes, I always stay away from that cottage. It's got history.'

Sophie drew in her breath. Here was her first lead.

'You mean the Baxters?'

'I don't know, do I?' The woman frowned.

'They were the people who lived there, the people who disappeared?'

'I don't know much about what happened at all, really.'

Sophie's heart sank as the prospect of her promising lead faded.

'Would you like a cup of tea, dear? I usually have one when I get back from shopping and it is a warm day.'

'That would be lovely. Thank you.'

'We can have it in the garden if you like.' She eyed up Bryony. 'Your dog might prefer to run around outside on such a nice afternoon?'

'She doesn't normally growl at strangers,' Sophie was quick to explain. 'She thought I was being threatened.'

'Well, if you could help me with my bags? My name's Mary Pritchard, by the way.'

'Sophie Blaze.'

'What an unusual name. Now where did I put my key? Ah, here it is. Come along in.'

'How long have you lived in Berkham?' Sophie asked as Mary unlocked the door.

'About ten years. I moved here after my husband died. The children had left home and I needed somewhere smaller. It's very nice although the character of the village has changed. It used to be young families and we had a village school, but when that closed the young people moved away. Now it's very quiet during the day. Do you know Berkham at all?'

'Not really, no.'

'So what brings you here?'

Mary's question created the perfect opening.

'I'm trying to track down the Baxters, Tony and Naomi?'

'And you say that was the name of the people who disappeared?'

'Yes.'

'Wasn't there a child involved too?'

'A son, Adam. He was little more than a baby, I believe.'

Mary put out a tray of biscuits. 'You'd better open the kitchen door, dear.' She eyed Bryony. Her over-active tail looked perilously close to sweeping the crockery off the dresser. 'Give your dog the run of the back garden. It's quite sheltered so she won't come to any harm.'

With a woof of delight Bryony trotted on to the terrace and was soon snuffling happily on the lawn. Mary turned her attention back to the jug kettle.

'The Baxters?' Sophie prompted.

'Ah yes.' Mary filled the teapot. 'I'm

not sure I can help you very much.' She stirred the pot. Sophie carried the tray on to the terrace for her and put it down on a garden table. 'Why do you want to find them?'

Sophie related her prepared story and was pleased Mary seemed to accept it at face value.

'If you like, I can ask around? Somebody may remember something, although it was a long time ago.'

'I wouldn't want to be a nuisance.' Sophie sipped at her tea.

If there was a can of worms to be unearthed, Sophie would rather Mary wasn't involved. In her experience sometimes the most innocent of questions could provoke an unpleasant reaction.

'It does seem strange, doesn't it, for a whole family to completely disappear with no evidence as to what happened to them?' Mary was speaking again.

'I agree,' Sophie replied.

'I've just had a thought.' Mary waved her biscuit in the air. 'Old Mrs Crampton. Nothing went on in the village without her knowing about it.'

'Who is Mrs Crampton?'

'She used to be the village post-mistress. She knew absolutely everybody.'

'She sounds an ideal lead. If you tell me where she lives, I could perhaps call in on her?' Sophie suggested.

Mary shook her head. 'She moved to a residential home to be nearer her daughter two years ago, but she used to live at number five, on the far side of the Baxters.'

'I suppose she would have been interviewed by the police at the time?'

'It's possible, but you know how it is, sometimes you don't remember every-thing that happened on a certain day and you get a bit muddled, then later, well, it's too late? Or perhaps you didn't like the policeman because he was asking awkward questions?'

'Exactly,' Sophie agreed with Mary, knowing full well the challenges of inter-viewing techniques. If an interviewee didn't take to you, then no amount of probing would get the right answers.

'Do you do this for a living?'

'Do what?' Mary's question took Sophie by surprise.

'Private investigation work.'

Sophie coughed as a biscuit crumb caught in her throat. Mary wasn't as naïve as she'd taken her for.

'I, er, well, yes,' she admitted.

Mary nodded. 'Thought so. I used to work for the police; not as a serving officer,' she was quick to add. 'I was a civilian. My work was on the secretarial side of things, but I was always interested in the unsolved cases. Some of the reports that came across my desk would make your hair stand on end. I remember once . . . '

'Well, er, thank you for the tea.' Sophie looked round for Bryony. Much as she enjoyed talking to Mary, she suspected she could be a bit of a gossip and Sophie had always found it was best to maintain as much professional discretion as possible.

'You're leaving already?' Mary looked disappointed.

'I have other leads to follow.' Sophie tempered her words with a warm smile.

When she didn't have her tape recorder with her she liked to write up her notes as soon as possible before something vital slipped her mind. Although it was early days in her investigation, she had the suspicion that there was a lot more hanging on this enquiry than Emma had let on and the sooner Sophie got things clearer in her mind the better. Sophie also suspected that if she didn't cut this interview short she could be in for a lengthy session of local gossip.

'Of course,' Mary smiled back at her. 'If there's anything I can do, let me know.'

'You don't have an address for Mrs Crampton?' Sophie asked.

'I'm afraid not, dear. Her daughter sometimes visits a friend in the village. If you leave me your details, I could contact you?'

Bryony settled down on the back seat of the car as Sophie drove out of the village. She contemplated dropping in on Emma on her way home, to update her on the day's progress, but she wasn't sure if she'd be working at the studio and Sophie didn't relish the idea of leaving a message with Jack West.

Sophie gave herself a mental shake as she drove along. What was she thinking of? Wanting to wimp out on a professional visit because she couldn't face Jack West?

That sort of behaviour was not on her agenda. Emma Mountjoy, not Jack West, was Sophie's client and Emma had asked for regular updates. A client's instructions were paramount and Sophie always saw them through to the letter. Unpleasant car mechanics must not be allowed to stand in her way.

She eased up on the accelerator as she approached the turn into the Stable Yard. An expensive sports car roared down the drive and sped out of the entrance, scattering small stones in its wake.

Sophie's eyebrows met her floppy

fringe and she choked as the car disappeared in a roar of exhaust fumes. She hadn't been able to identify the driver, but there had been no doubt in her mind as to the identity of the passenger. It had been Emma Mount-joy.

A Confrontation With Jack

'Still spying on innocent people?' Jack's voice through the open driver's window caught Sophie at a disadvantage. She hadn't heard him approach and it made her jump. Bryony thumped her tail on the back seat then nosed forward to lick Jack's hand, an honour she rarely dispensed to a stranger on a first meeting.

'I have every right to be here,' Sophie said, wishing she'd spotted Jack first and that Bryony wasn't quite so enthusiastic with her greeting.

'A word in your ear,' Jack leaned forward, distractedly stroking Bryony's head.

Sophie tried not to notice the deep brown colour of his eyes. If the circumstances hadn't been so confrontational she would have enjoyed the experience of smiling at him just for the pleasure of seeing his face crease back at her with his endearingly crooked smile. As it was his assumption that she was again snooping on Emma was making her angry.

'No,' she corrected him before he could continue. She was pleased to see a flare of surprise in the brown eyes. 'Let me give you a word of warning in your ear, Mr West. If you continue harassing me in this manner I shall take steps to ensure that the appropriate authorities are made aware of your behaviour.'

'You'll do what?' He gaped at her.

Sophie opened her mouth to repeat her threat, a threat she had no intention of carrying out, but she absolutely refused to be intimidated by the likes of Jack West and the sooner he became aware of that fact the better.

'Daddy,' a voice wailed from the van parked on the grass verge behind Sophie.

Jack straightened up immediately.

'Coming,' he called out.

Sophie glimpsed a sturdy body in her wing mirror. The child was dressed in boot camp shorts and tee shirt and looked decidedly grubby.

'I'm hungry,' he complained as he hung out of the van passenger seat window, 'and you promised me chips for tea.'

'Sit down at once, Harry, before you fall.'

The little boy catching sight of Sophie beamed and waved. The resemblance was impossible to mistake. The two males possessed the same colour eyes, curly hair and pugnacious jaw line.

'Hello.' The child revealed several gaps in his teeth as he smiled at Sophie. 'My name's Harry West.'

'Mine's Sophie.'

'I'm five. What's your dog's name?'

'Bryony.'

'Do you like chips?' With all the single-mindedness of a small boy, Harry switched subjects. His behaviour reminded Sophie of her young nephews.

'I love them,' Sophie smiled back at him.

'Emma won't eat them. She says they make you fat so when she and Daddy have dinner together, he has to pretend to like all sorts of horrible green salady stuff. Yuk.' Harry giggled behind his hand. 'Last night when he came home he filled up on an enormous slice of chocolate cake.'

'Harry, please.' Harry ignored his father's interruption and Sophie followed his example.

'My mother makes a lovely chocolate cake,' she confided to Harry.

'Does she?'

'Yup, so that's another thing we have in common,' Sophie replied, still determinedly ignoring the expression on Jack's face.

Harry's little face lit up. 'Emma's gone out tonight with her boyfriend, so we're going to the chippy. Do you and Bryony want to come?'

'Harry,' Jack snapped back at his son, 'I've told you already, get back into your seat.'

Harry raised his eyebrows. 'Are you cross 'cos Emma didn't invite you to go with them?' he asked.

Sophie couldn't resist turning her attention back to Jack. 'Are you?' she enquired, a dimple denting her cheek.

'No, I'm not.'

'And is that an exclusive?'

'If one word of what my son has let slip appears in print, there'll be trouble,' Jack warned her.

'What sort of trouble?'

'There's such a thing as invasion of privacy.'

'I wasn't aware I had invaded anybody's privacy,' Sophie countered back at him, 'and may I remind you it was you who challenged me in the first place?'

'No, I didn't.'

'Yes, you did. You accused me of snooping round your lock up and you are now parked on the grass verge behind me and invading my body space by ranting on about all sorts of things I'm supposed to have been up to.' Sophie pushed on for good measure, 'The editor of the local newspaper is not going to like this one little bit.'

'He's not going to know about it — is

he?' Jack countered back uncertainly.

'Actually, he's a she, yes, we girls get everywhere, don't we?' Sophie was enjoying herself hugely as she continued. 'And I could be persuaded not to tell her what I know,' Sophie informed Jack, 'if you apologise to me nicely. Otherwise Harry could be reading all about his father on next week's front page.'

'Leave my son out of this.' Jack began to look angry and Sophie felt slightly ashamed of her empty threat. Jack was right. It wasn't fair to involve the child. Something was also telling her it wouldn't do to push Jack West too far. There was a stubborn thrust to his chin that could prove difficult to deal with.

'Is the lady coming with us, Daddy?' Harry butted into the silence.

'No, she isn't,' Jack replied through clenched teeth.

'That's a pity,' Sophie sighed. 'I find prying on people gives you a tremendous appetite.'

'I don't know what game you're

playing, Miss Blaze,' a small muscle tugged at the corner of his eye as he tried to control his annoyance, 'but let me inform you I have no intention of giving in to your blackmail. Neither do I intend apologising for my behaviour so the next move is up to you.'

'I take it dinner's off then, is it?'

'If you'll excuse me,' Jack ignored the taunt, 'I have to look after my son.'

'I'll see you tomorrow,' Sophie called after him as he turned on his heel.

She watched him make his way back to his van. She hadn't noticed his slight limp before. She bit her lip, already regretting some of the things she had said.

'Daddy, can we have a dog like Bryony?'

Sophie did not hear Jack's reply as he clambered into the van. A chubby fist was waved in goodbye as Jack started up and drove off in the direction of the chip shop.

Sophie watched the van disappear from sight, a thoughtful frown drawing her eyebrows together. Why was Jack so uptight and why did he keep accusing her of snooping on Emma? What was it Emma had to hide?

Sophie began to suspect her client hadn't been totally upfront with her about her reason for wanting to trace what had happened to the Baxters. But why was Jack West sounding off at her at every opportunity? They had only met twice and each time he'd accused her of mounting a stakeout on Emma.

Perhaps he was trying to protect himself. Was Jack's wife aware of their close relationship and the intimate suppers her husband shared with Emma Mountjoy? Was that the reason he was so twitchy? Were they having an affair? Did he suspect her of spying on him as well?

Sophie didn't think so. Harry had mentioned Emma's boyfriend and had been quite free talking about her. Was it Emma's boyfriend who'd driven out of the gates as if the hounds of hell were on his tail?

'I vaguely remember the Baxter case,' Mark Blaze admitted to his daughter over dinner. 'There were rumours at the time about Tony Baxter.'

'What sort of rumours?'

'He worked for the Council I think, in the planning department. It was something to do with irregular transactions.'

'You mean bribes?'

Mark grimaced. 'No-one ever said as much, but one or two applications were rubber-stamped with fast track ease. I don't think anything ever came of the enquiries and I don't know what happened in the end. I wasn't really involved in the case. What's brought all this up again?' he asked.

'Client confidentiality,' Sophie said, as she licked the last of the custard off her dessertspoon. 'No-one makes apple pie as good as yours, Mum,' she said.

'There's some left over, dear. You can take it back to your flat with you if you like.'

'What about me?' Sophie's father grumbled. 'Don't I get seconds?'

'We only have desserts once a week and you need to watch your figure.'

Mark Blaze made a face. 'You shouldn't be such a good cook,' he grumbled.

'And you should take more exercise.'

Sophie listened to her parents' banter as she helped her mother clear away the dishes.

'Need any help with the washing up?' her father called through after he'd shaken the crumbs from the tablecloth.

'Yes,' Sophie said.

'No,' her mother insisted. 'It's quicker if we do it and there's something I want to talk to you about.'

'I'll water my tomato plants then.' Mark Blaze seized the opportunity to make a quick getaway into the garden. 'Come on, Bryony,' he clicked his fingers, 'come and help me.'

Bryony pattered out onto the terrace behind him.

'If it's about a new boyfriend, Mum,

there's no-one on the horizon. It's not easy keeping up a relationship when you work the hours I do. Besides, Tom and Sam have already provided you with more than enough grandchildren.'

Janet Blaze's face softened.

'Tom's twins are so sweet. You should have seen them dressed in their little ballet dresses last week and Sam's brood of boys are very keen on football. They quite exhausted Mark last time they visited.'

'There you are then,' Sophie wiped up a plate. 'There's no need for me to do anything on that front for a while.'

'Actually that wasn't what I wanted to talk to you about.'

'What was it then?'

'Emma Mountjoy.'

The plate Sophie was holding nearly slipped out of her fingers.

'Careful, dear,' her mother admonished her, 'that plate is part of a set.'

Sophie frowned. She was always scrupulous about protecting her clients' identities. Had she let Emma's name slip while they were talking about the Baxters? She didn't think so.

'What about her — Emma?' she prompted her mother.

'Wasn't she the girl who was so unkind to you at school?'

'She was games captain,' Sophie admitted.

'That's the one.' Janet Blaze wiped her hands on her apron. 'Now where did I put it?'

'Put what?'

'It was only a snippet in my magazine, but Mountjoy is quite an unusual name isn't it? And it does mention a connection with Steepways.' Janet adjusted her glasses. 'Here we are.' She thrust the article at Sophie.

'I don't understand,' Sophie looked up after she'd read it. 'Who is Iain Buchanan?'

'He's a major character in a soap opera about a health club. I only watch it when your father's watering his vegetables or out at his club. He says it's all too far fetched to be believable but I enjoy it. Anyway, Iain Buchanan has been tipped for a part in a major film.'

'And he's going out with Emma Mountjoy?'

'It doesn't actually say it's your friend,' Janet admitted, 'but he's been spotted out together with a girl of the same name and I wondered if you knew anything about it?'

'Nothing at all. Why should I?' Sophie replied.

'You went to the same school.'

'We didn't keep in touch after I left.'

'She mixed with the horsey set, didn't she?' Janet smiled at her daughter as she flicked the switch on the jug kettle. 'Not really our scene. All the same, it's quite a coincidence, isn't it?'

'It is indeed,' Sophie agreed as she began sorting out the coffee cups. 'Could you do me a favour, Mum?' she asked. 'Could you record the next episode of your soap opera for me?'

'It's on tonight.'

'Good. I'd like to see what this Iain Buchanan looks like.'

'Now, there is some chocolate cake left over from the weekend.' Janet produced the remains of her Sunday afternoon tea. 'We could have a slice with our coffee?'

'That would be lovely, Mum,' Sophie agreed. 'And I'll take an extra piece home with me too, if that's OK?'

'Are you having a tea party?'

'Let's just say I know a young gentleman who might appreciate a slice. I'm afraid he's only about five years old,' she added before the light of hope in her mother's eyes could gain ground.

'Of course, dear,' she added looking round for a cake tin. 'Go and fetch your father but give me a few moments to set the recorder.'

The two women exchanged a conspiratorial smile before Sophie strolled onto the patio in search of her father. If what her mother suspected was true, Sophie now understood why Jack West was so twitchy. Emma was dating a media star. But it still didn't explain why Emma hadn't told her about it in the first place.

'Coffee,' Sophie semaphored to her father as he looked up from watering his tomatoes.

Her next update meeting with Emma she decided was going to be very interesting.

Sophie Meets A Star

'My name's Iain Buchanan.' The perma-tanned man stepped forward, smiled and held out his hand with all the practised ease of someone accustomed to being in the public eye.

Sophie could see why he was such a hit with the ladies. He would look totally at home escorting a starlet down the red carpet at film premieres. He possessed the type of rugged good looks tinged with a touch of urban charm and a roguish twinkle in his eye that would go down well with all the ladies, from teenagers to young professionals and grandmothers. Sophie hadn't yet had the chance to look at her mother's video of the latest episode of the soap opera he starred in, but she now understood why the press were so interested in following his career and his love life.

'This is Sophie Blaze.' Emma appeared

at his elbow and linked her arm through Iain's. 'We're old school friends.'

Iain raised an eyebrow. 'Really?'

Sophie blushed under his scrutiny. The day was warm and she had decided to wear a flowery T shirt and floaty long skirt. The look was definitely Bohemian. Emma was chic and casual in tailored chinos and crisp white blouse.

'Emma was sports captain,' Sophie explained, not wishing to compromise Emma by admitting that describing them as friends was stretching the truth a bit.

'You don't look the horsey sort to me,' Iain replied, his eyes lingering over Sophie's floaty skirt.

'Not all my friends ride,' Emma interjected crisply.

'Of course not, darling.' He smiled at her. 'Well, Sophie Blaze, I'm pleased to meet you. Is this a social call?' he asked casually.

Sophie caught the fleeting expression of panic in Emma's eyes and took pity on her friend.

'It's professional,' she said, sticking to her policy of adhering as closely to the truth at possible. It was obvious Emma did not want the real reason behind their relationship to be revealed and Sophie was prepared to go along with her feelings. 'I'm helping Emma with a project.'

'Yes,' Emma gushed, picking up her cue, 'Sophie's my temporary assistant. There are one or two things I need sorting out in my personal life, things to do with my father's estate, actually, and I'm so busy these days, I don't have the time to see to them.'

'Understood.' Iain cleared his throat and looked expectantly at Sophie. 'Do you watch television?' he asked when she didn't speak.

'Not very often,' Sophie admitted. 'I often work unsociable hours and while everyone else is relaxing I'm usually out and about.'

'What exactly does a temporary personal assistant do?' he asked.

This was a sticky question but Sophie

was used to thinking on her feet.

'I'm a sort of Jill of all trades.'

'That must be interesting.'

'It is.'

Sophie wished Iain would let the subject drop and that Emma would come to her rescue.

'No two days are the same, I should imagine.'

'Sophie decided to work for herself,' Emma explained. 'She wanted to go into the police but didn't pass the medical.'

'I'm mildly colour blind,' Sophie added.

'Really? Hey, we may schedule that into a storyline,' Iain said, then looked expectantly at Sophie.

'Er, Iain is currently starring in a television series.' Emma looked faintly embarrassed when Sophie didn't respond.

'I see,' she said.

Iain looked disappointed over Sophie's lack of reaction to this piece of news. So too did Emma but Sophie wasn't one to pander to celebrity, not that she had met many famous people. Her parents had always taught her to accept people for who they were, no matter what they did for a living or where they came from.

'Yes, and there are one or two things going on in his life right now that are a bit hush hush so you didn't see him here?' Emma raised her voice as if asking a question.

'I'm sure we can rely on your friend not to go babbling to the press about me,' Iain said with a deprecating smile that almost suggested he wouldn't be too fussed if she did.

'And I'm sure Emma will tell you on our old school friend's honour that I can be very discreet.' Sophie looked pointedly at Emma. A faint blush stained the base of her friend's neck.

Through the open window Sophie could hear what sounded like Jack working on a car. There had been no sign of him earlier when she had driven into the compound. Sophie was beginning to wish she had telephoned Emma before calling in on her. She had wanted to have a private word about the rumours circulating in the press. A quick trawl of her local newsagents had revealed that Iain was a big name in the celeb market and no gossip magazine was complete without an article on him. Sophie had not expected to find Iain Buchanan drinking coffee in Emma's studio and discussing plans for their forthcoming marriage. She had not realised the romance was so far advanced.

'Is that your mechanic friend making all that noise?' Iain asked, picking up on the metallic clang of machinery.

'I expect so. He usually arrives about now after he drops Harry off at school.'

Iain nodded. 'He seems to hang around here a lot. Anyone would think you and he were an item.'

'I look after his son, Harry, some-times,' Emma fiddled with a stray strand of her hair. 'We go back a long way, Iain, I've told you about him before.'

'Sorry to be so touchy, but you know

how it is, sweetheart. I don't want the studio finding out about any scandal,' Iain explained to Sophie. 'I've signed a decency clause in my contract to that effect. That's why Emma and I have to keep our relationship a secret.'

'Emma's not a scandal, nor is she indecent,' Sophie protested on her friend's behalf. Her remark earned a grateful glance from Emma who was looking as uneasy as Sophie felt.

'I'm not saying she is,' Iain's voice was treacle smooth, 'but the studio is very controlling. In the past they've been caught out by some of the more scandalous revelations about their stars in certain sections of the press and now they're hyper about absolutely anything.'

'I see,' Sophie said quietly, glad her life was sufficiently low key to be of absolutely no interest to any high powered studio mogul. She couldn't imagine anything worse than to have to keep looking over her shoulder in case someone was watching her.

'So there's nothing for me to worry

about regarding you and Jack?' Iain probed returning his attention back to Emma.

'We share the occasional television supper,' she confessed, 'and in the past we dated once or twice,' she rushed on, 'but it's been over for ages. Jack still likes to keep an eye on me, but these days our relationship is that of good friends.'

'As long as it is over.' Iain finished his coffee.

'Of course it is. Our current relationship is purely platonic and usually concerns Harry.'

'Shouldn't that be his mother's concern?' Iain asked.

'Jack's a single parent. Linda died in an accident.'

Sophie murmured, 'How sad.'

'Actually, I introduced them. We met up at a disco and I knew Jack because he liked to help my uncle out while he was still at school. You know he owned a garage, my uncle, I mean? Anyway, Linda and I went out one evening and Jack was there and the rest, as they say, is history.' Emma's smile was tinged with sadness. 'Jack doesn't really talk about Linda now. Harry was only a baby when the accident happened.'

A ringing tone from Iain's mobile interrupted their conversation. He fished it out of a pocket in his leather jacket and strolled away from the two girls to take the call.

Emma shook her head at Sophie when she tried to ask another question.

'Not now,' she put a hand to her lips.

Iain finished speaking on the phone. 'I've got to go,' he said.

'It's your day off,' Emma protested. 'I've rescheduled all my appointments. We were going to look at rings.'

'Sorry,' Iain apologised, 'my agent has just received a call. I'm needed for a second audition for that film part we're going after. It doesn't do to hang around in these circumstances. The competition is too fierce. I'll call you tonight, darling.' He kissed Emma's cheek. 'Nice to meet you, er, Suzie.'

'You too, er, Angus,' Sophie couldn't help retaliating.

Her childish gesture earned her a frown from Emma.

'Sorry,' she mouthed at her friend.

Iain smiled at both girls before disappearing down the staircase and out into the yard outside. Sophie heard a hurried exchange between him and Jack before the powerful thrust of an exhaust indicated that Iain had started up his car. Neither girl spoke until the throb of the engine had faded away into the distance.

'Can I speak now?' Sophie asked.

'You shouldn't tease him,' Emma chided her with a twinkle in her eye. 'All actors have fragile egos.'

'As well as bad memories for names?'

'I would have told you about Iain earlier,' Emma began to explain, 'only you can see how it is. The less people who know about us the better.'

'At least it explains why Jack West treats me as though I've got the plague,' Sophie replied.

'Jack?' Emma looked surprised. 'He's a pussy cat.'

'Are we talking about the same Jack West?' It was Sophie's turn to chide her friend.

'My neighbour in unit 6B?'

'Well, your neighbour in unit 6B thinks I'm some sort of paparazzi who has taken to hanging around your studio, hoping to get a glimpse of you and your boyfriend.'

Emma burst into laughter at the look of disgust on Sophie's face. It was so infectious Sophie found herself joining in.

'That's ridiculous,' Emma dabbed at the corner of her eyes.

'I know that and you know that, but Jack doesn't.'

'You don't know anything about that sort of world.'

'Try telling Jack West. He's accosted me twice and neither time was it a pleasant experience.'

'He's only got my interests at heart. I think he sees himself as the defender of my honour.'

'How very *knight in shining armour*.'

Sophie began to wonder if Emma had been entirely truthful about the nature of her relationship with Jack.

'Would you like me to have a word with him for you?' Emma volunteered.

Sophie shook her head. 'I'll tell him in my own good time.'

'He knows about me and Iain, of course, but not about the engagement, so I'd be grateful if you kept that under your hat.'

'Sure. No problem.' Sophie hesitated. 'About what you said,' she began.

'When?'

'Just now, you and Jack. I don't mean to pry, but maybe I should know?'

Emma shrugged. 'About the true nature of our relationship? There's not much to tell. We've enjoyed a couple of dinner dates and a visit to the cinema, that sort of thing. It was over before it had begun. I was feeling low because of Daddy and then I lost my uncle too. Jack was lonely. We were mutual shoulders to cry on I suppose. There's never been any chemistry between us.

At the risk of sounding corny, we're just good friends.'

'I'm not sure Iain believed you.'

'He has to be so careful about everything. The studio is constantly on his back making sure he sticks to every condition of his contract. That's why I didn't tell you about him. I'm sorry. It's not that I didn't trust you.'

'Do you still want me to go on with my investigations into the Baxters?'

'I'd almost forgotten about them, but I think I do,' Emma nodded. 'You see, if Daddy was hiding anything in his past, it's better I know about it before some press hound gets hold of the story and blows it out of all proportion.'

'Do you think your father could possibly have known Naomi Baxter?' Sophie asked.

'I'm not sure. He had one or two lady friends after Mummy re-married, but I never really got to know them. How are your enquiries going?'

'I think I've got a tentative lead. The lady who ran the local post office seemed to know everything that went on. She doesn't live in the village any more, but her daughter still visits a friend. I've left my details with a neighbour who says she'll pass them on.'

'Fine. I'll leave it all up to you then.'

Emma undid her hair clasp and shook it free.

'That's better. I hate the honed and toned girlfriend image, but I have to do it every time Iain calls round.'

'Why?'

'In case the studio finds out about us.'

'Tell me to mind my own business if you don't want to answer,' Sophie began.

'Go on,' Emma replied.

'Are you really going to marry Iain Buchanan?'

The light dusting of freckles on Emma's nose joined up in a very becoming blush. She giggled like a schoolgirl.

'Of course. Don't you think he's the most wonderful man in the world?'

Sophie made a noise at the back of her throat. She suspected that Emma wouldn't be interested in her honest reply. Iain Buchanan was far too image conscious for Sophie's liking. She also suspected that with two such volatile egos in constant confrontation there were lively times ahead in Emma and Iain's relationship.

'Congratulations,' Sophie replied by way of an answer.

'We had hoped to go away somewhere quiet to get married but Iain suspects the story may break before we could get round to it, so we thought if I had a ring to show everyone the studio would take our relationship seriously.'

'Where did you meet?' Sophie asked.

'He came to my friend's stables because he needed to learn to ride for a storyline. It was the most amazing thing. We took one look at each other . . . '

'And saw stars?'

'You wait until it happens to you,' Emma insisted, 'then you'll know what

I'm talking about.'

'I'll take your word for it.' Sophie looked round for her bag.

Emma uncovered her latest piece of work. 'Better get on with this I suppose,' she said.

'Is it all right if I still call in on a casual basis?' Sophie asked.

'Sure, and I meant what I said about Jack.'

'Sorry?' Sophie found her bag and flung it over her shoulder.

'You can leave any messages with him. Like I said he's a pussycat once you get to know him properly,' Emma insisted.

'Would that be as in a tiger?' she asked, adding, 'one who hasn't been fed for days?'

'If I didn't know better,' Emma said from behind her easel, 'I'd suspect you and Jack are attracted to each other.'

Sophie widened her blue eyes in horror.

'Whatever gave you that idea?'

'Every time I mention his name you

come to life and I know what I'm talking about. It's my job to paint emotion.'

'Well this time your instinct has let
you down big time,' Sophie replied.

'I don't think so,' Emma daubed a
streak of vermilion onto her canvas.

Sophie Bonds With Harry

When Sophie got back to her flat the answer phone was flashing indicating a call was received while she was out.

'Miss Blaze?' It was Mary Pritchard's voice. 'Good news and bad news, I'm afraid. Mrs Crampton passed away at Easter so unfortunately you won't be able to talk to her. However,' Mary paused for dramatic effect, 'I bumped into Irene Bell in Berkham today. You remember I told you she still had a friend here? Irene is Mrs Crampton's daughter. Sorry, I should have told you that before. I'm not used to machines. They always get me in a muddle.'

Sophie sighed, wondering if and when Mary was going to get to the point. 'Well, anyway,' Mary continued, 'I gave her your details because she said she is still going through her mother's things. Mrs Crampton used to hoard diaries and letters so there may be a lead there. I don't know if Irene will be in touch but that's all we can do, really, isn't it? So nice to have met you the other day.'

Mary made a few more comments about the weather and Bryony before clearing the line.

After making some coffee and settling down in front of her television, Sophie watched her mother's videoed episode of the soap starring Iain Buchanan. She had stayed on chatting to her mother over coffee and by the time she had finally said goodbye Janet Blaze was able to slip the finished recording into her daughter's shoulder bag.

As far as Sophie could make out Iain played the manager of a health club that was attached to an upmarket hotel. His duties did not appear too onerous and a lot of his time seemed to be spent supervising glamorous young assistants, several of whom were dressed in attractive swimsuits and had figures to die for. They also suffered an alarming amount of personal problems that Iain was doing his best to sort out. The rest of the time he made smalltalk with the influential hotel guests who booked in for treatments and all the other services the club offered.

There appeared to be a permanent girlfriend in the background. Her jealousy over his contact with the wives of some of the male hotel guests fuelled several confrontational scenes. A sub plot concerned a jolly handyman and the cleaner who were involved in a mix up regarding cleaning fluids and something to do with the swimming pool. The water was threatening to turn an interesting shade of pink and the pool was going to have to be closed down pending further investigations. A swimming gala was scheduled for the next afternoon. The signature music cut into the cliff hanger ending.

Sophie realised she would have to be a regular viewer to understand exactly what was going on, but the plot lines didn't look too hard to follow.

What was obvious was Iain Buchanan's magnetism. His presence dominated every scene. The camera angles always flattered his profile and his character's genuine niceness came over as he tried to please everybody. Sophie could understand why he was being tipped for stardom. She could also understand why Emma and he wanted their engagement kept a secret. His legions of fans would be devastated over the news.

Despite Iain's affability on the screen, Sophie also suspected he was very career orientated and he wouldn't want anything getting in the way of his rumoured film deal. Poor old Emma, Sophie suspected, was destined to remain in the background.

She sincerely hoped her reading of the situation was correct and that Iain wasn't playing fast and loose with her school friend's affections. Although the two girls had little in common, Sophie would hate to see Emma dropped because she didn't fit in with a studio image.

Sophie flicked off the television switch and stretched. It had been a while since she'd taken Bryony for a jog on the common and she'd done nothing but sit around all day.

'Come on, Bryony.' She nudged the snoring dog. 'Joggies.'

★ ★ ★

The rattling of the letterbox woke Sophie the next morning. Surprised she had slept in so long, Sophie padded to the kitchen and juiced some fresh oranges then let Bryony out onto the patio before going in search of her post. A padded brown envelope lay on the mat. She frowned as she picked it up and turned it over. It was personally addressed to her but she didn't recognise the handwriting.

Settling down at the kitchen table she left the patio door open to enjoy the best of the warm sunshine. Her top floor flat faced south and on mornings like this the view stretched over the

Surrey hills, almost into the next county, but today she had no eyes for the sweeping landscape. Ignoring her freshly squeezed juice she undid the bulky envelope then read the letter accompanying the bundle of documents inside.

It was from Irene Bell, Mrs Crampton's daughter.

Dear Miss Blaze, it began,

Mary Pritchard gave me your details and I thought you might be interested in the enclosed documents. From what it says on the envelope, I gather my mother was looking after them on behalf of Naomi Baxter. She must have forgotten all about them as they were at the bottom of an old trunk. I was going to burn them as they are of no interest to me so please feel free to dispose of them as you wish.

The note was signed, *Irene Bell.*

Sophie undid the flap of the second

envelope. Several letters floated onto the table. They were yellowed with age and smelt musty. Sophie's fingers hovered over the nearest as she tried to remember what Emma had found amongst her father's effects. There had been the newspaper cuttings about Tony and Naomi's disappearance and a lock of child's hair.

Emma had insisted it wasn't hers.

Sophie was half way through reading the first letter before she realised it was of an extremely personal nature. Although there were large gaps in her knowledge base, it was obvious to Sophie that Naomi was thinking about setting up home on her own away from Tony. The writer of the letter was suggesting several suitable properties in the area. Sophie's hand shook as she skipped the more personal sections of the letter and turned it over to read the signature at the bottom.

It was that of Gerald Mountjoy, Emma's father.

Sophie felt as though she had swallowed a lump of lead. Emma's father and Naomi were close friends, so close that Naomi didn't want Tony reading their letters so she had given them to Mrs Crampton for safekeeping. They had lain forgotten for years in an old suitcase.

If the newspapers should get hold of this story and link it to Emma's relationship with Iain Buchanan then the ensuing scandal could have a disastrous effect. Iain would be deemed to have broken a clause in his contract and the film studio might withdraw their offer of a film part.

Sophie's mouth was parched. She drank the whole of her glass of orange juice as she wondered what to do next. If the only evidence of the affair was the bundle of letters Mrs Crampton had been looking after, then the chances of anyone finding out about Emma's father's involvement with Naomi Baxter were slim.

The telephone rang interrupting her thoughts.

'Sophie?' It was her father speaking.

'Hello, Dad.' She did her best to keep her voice normal.

'Glad I've caught you in. I bumped into an old colleague in town who I used to work with and I mentioned the Baxter case to him. He remembered it quite well.'

'Go on,' she urged her father.

'The general opinion was that Tony Baxter might have been in trouble at work so he fled abroad and took his sister and her son with him.'

'Naomi was his sister? Not his wife?'

'Not according to my colleague. The investigation was scaled down when no further evidence came to light.'

'Thanks, Dad.' Sophie hung up on her call.

This was one of the times when her work presented a challenge. Should she tell Emma everything she had discovered or should she be economical with the truth? Emma had a right to know of course, she had paid for Sophie's services. On the other hand if Sophie gave Emma the paperwork there was a chance that it might wind up in the wrong hands. Emma was a tad on the scatty side, Sophie remembered and quite likely to leave important papers lying about.

Sophie bit her lip then with a quick look of apology at Bryony who had thumped her tail hopefully on the edge of her basket Sophie scooped up all her paperwork and stuffed it into her shoulder bag. No matter how painful the news, Emma had to know. It was the only professional decision Sophie could take and there was no time like the present.

Five minutes later she was driving past Bill at the gate of the industrial estate. He waved and indicated he would sign her in. She drove past him and parked her car in one of the bays and out of the way of the delivery vehicles. She didn't want Jack West accusing her of blocking him in.

Striding along the walkway towards Emma's studio she heard a voice calling out to her.

'Hello. Where's your dog?'

'Harry?' Her footsteps faltered as the little boy bounded over, a beaming smile of welcome on his face.

'You haven't got your dog with you,' he repeated.

'I had to leave her at home,' Sophie explained. 'She'd get in the way here. Where's your daddy?' she asked.

'Don't know.'

Sophie frowned. The double doors fronting unit 6B were padlocked shut.

'Is he out?' she asked Harry.

''Spect so,' Harry replied jumping up and down in a puddle.

'Shouldn't Emma be looking after you?'

'She's out too,' Harry said, spying another puddle and running over to it.

'Isn't there any school today?'

'Training.'

Sophie glanced up at Emma's workshop. It was in darkness.

'Let's go and see Bill on the gate, shall we?' Sophie suggested putting out a hand.

Harry's hand was plump and warm as he clutched hers.

'Bill?' Sophie tapped on his window.

He slid it back. 'Hello there, young man.' He glanced down at Harry. 'What are you doing here?'

'Waiting for Daddy.'

'I found him,' Sophie explained, 'outside Jack's unit. It's all locked up and Emma's out too.'

Bill glanced at his log. 'Miss Mountjoy hasn't come in yet. If she worked late last night then she probably wouldn't arrive that early this morning. Mr West,' he ran his finger down the entries, 'had an urgent call out about an hour ago. No idea when he'll be back.'

'Who normally drops Harry off at school?'

'Mr West usually does it on his way in.'

'Do you have a spare key to his unit?'

'I do, but I can't let you in — health and safety,' Bill explained. 'If anything should happen it would be my responsibility. And I can't really look after Harry until his father gets back. There's too much going on, especially if there's a delivery. I wouldn't be able to keep an eye on him and it would mean leaving him on his own and I don't think that's allowed either.'

'Can I come home with you, Sophie?' Harry asked. 'I could play with your dog. I won't get in the way, I promise.'

'You could leave a message with me,' Bill suggested, 'and I'll give it to Mr West the moment he gets back.'

'I was hoping to see Miss Mountjoy on a matter of business.'

'I could give her a message too, if you like as soon as she gets in.'

Realising she had no other choice, Sophie scribbled her telephone number down on Bill's pad.

'I'm hungry,' Harry complained, sitting on one of her nephew's booster seats, which always lived in the back of Sophie's car.

'Fancy some chips?' Sophie suggested as she jumped into the driving seat, 'and chocolate cake?'

'Please. Won't this be an exciting adventure to tell Daddy? He doesn't let me have chips during the day.'

'Today's different,' Sophie insisted. 'We'll treat it as a holiday.'

Bryony launched into Harry as he tumbled through the door of Sophie's flat. While she busied herself getting chips out of the freezer and warming them up in the oven then sorting out a soft drink and a slice of chocolate cake for Harry, Bryony and Harry played a noisy happy ball game. Sophie was reluctant to let the child have the run of the patio as her flat was on the top floor, so the ball bounced around the floor getting in everyone's way.

'Chips are ready,' Sophie served up two portions on the warmed plates.

Her breakfast orange juice had been a long while ago and she and Harry whose face was liberally covered in chocolate icing tucked in hungrily.

'I saw that,' Sophie scolded Harry as he slipped Bryony a chip when he thought she wasn't looking.

Harry giggled. 'I only gave her one,' he explained.

'No more then as they're not good for her. She'll get fat.'

'You eat chips and you're not fat,' Harry said as he squirted more tomato sauce onto his plate.

'That's because I make sure we get lots of exercise.'

'You're more fun than Emma,' Harry informed Sophie.

A smile tugged the corner of Sophie's mouth at these young words of wisdom.

'Am I?'

'She doesn't like getting dirty so she won't play with me.'

Sophie looked down in dismay at her T shirt. It was covered in a mixture of dirt from a bouncing ball, tomato sauce that had missed its target and a greasy chip smear. Her jeans too had suffered from Harry's enthusiastic puddle jumping and were covered in dried mud.

A dripping noise from the other end of the table alerted Sophie to the fact that Harry's juice glass was rolling across the table towards her. She was too late to prevent it landing in her lap, together with the last of the melted chocolate cake.

'Sorry,' Harry scrambled out of his seat with a giggle. 'My fingers slipped. I'll get it.'

Bryony began to bark as Harry slid onto the floor to pick up his now empty glass from under the cooker.

'Harry, no,' Sophie said, 'you'll get your hand stuck.'

'Won't,' he insisted as he wriggled about.

Sophie slipped on more orange juice as she crouched down beside him. A warm woof in her ear made her jump. Harry giggled again as she lost her balance and fell onto her bottom. From her prone position on the floor her nose crashed into a pair of industrial length work boots.

'Daddy,' Harry squealed and launched himself into his father's arms. 'I've been eating chips because today's a holiday and they don't make Sophie fat, do they? So Emma's wrong, isn't she?'

The Mystery Deepens

By now Sophie's hair, never well behaved at the best of times, had worked itself loose and she could feel it slipping out of its scrunchie. Curly tendrils of her misbehaving locks tickled the side of her face. She wasn't sure, but she suspected her appearance resembled that of a scarecrow having an extra bad hair day.

'Let me help you up,' Jack offered in a voice that didn't sound a bit like his normal one. It sounded lighter, as if he found the situation amusing. Sophie's flush of embarrassment deepened. This was not the professional image she liked to portray, especially not when Jack West was around.

The touch of his hand was firm against hers as he hauled her to her feet.

'Thank you,' she gasped, attempting to repair the damage to her hair.

She caught a glimpse of her reflection in the mirror and stifled a gasp. Scarecrow would have been too mild a word to use to describe her appearance. She had a blob of chocolate icing stuck on the end of her nose and a stray chip appeared to have attached itself to her scrunchie and was now dangling by her left ear. She swiped it away. It landed on Jack's boot.

'Come on, Harry, out of the way,' Jack addressed his son who was gaping wide eyed at the scene unfolding before his eyes.

'Sophie and I were playing, Daddy,' he explained, 'and then I spilt my drink. Sorry. Sophie was brilliant but she slipped over. It wasn't her fault,' he admitted manfully.

Sophie's heart warmed to the little boy. Young as he was he was trying to take responsibility for the disaster.

'I can see that.' Jack's expression softened as he took in his son's grubby face.

'I was drawing. Look.'

Harry held up a sheet of Sophie's notepaper on which he'd coloured in a garish picture of Bryony, enormous eyed and panting. Her pink tongue had taken on a monstrous glow. Harry had not held back on the colour detail.

'Very nice, but you're in the way, old chap.'

With much manoeuvring of positions and on Sophie's behalf, a reluctance to have more physical contact with Jack than was absolutely necessary, she managed to sit down in the chair recently vacated by Harry.

Without being asked to Jack cleared up the mess on the kitchen floor, removed the cold chip from his boot, wiped down the table then organised more drinks from the bottle of juice in the fridge while Sophie rubbed at her nose with a damp tissue and disentangled another chip from her hair.

'There you are. Hope you don't mind me helping myself?' Jack closed the fridge door with a gentle click, 'only you do look as though you could use some more refreshment.'

'Thank you.' Sophie cooled her hands around the iced glass he thrust towards her. She knew her nose was probably shining like an over active beacon. It always did when she rubbed it.

He pulled out the chair opposite Sophie and Harry returned his attention to his drawing, scribbling more felt pen colour onto Bryony's patches.

'How did you get in?' Sophie asked after she'd eased the dryness in her throat.

'The door was on the latch. Anyone could have walked in.'

'Everyone's pretty casual about that sort of thing round here,' Sophie explained.

When they'd arrived back at the flat, she'd had her hands full looking after Harry and an over exuberant Bryony and she'd totally forgotten to attend to the front door.

'I called out, but I couldn't make myself heard above the racket my son was making.'

'Bryony was barking too, Daddy,' Harry butted in.

Jack stroked his son's untidy hair. 'Have you thanked Sophie for looking after you?'

'Course I have, I think,' he added uncertainly.

Sophie could feel her skin redden over Jack's use of her first name.

'It was my pleasure,' she mumbled.

'Bill gave me your message,' Jack said after they took a few moments out to sip their drinks.

'Did he explain what happened?'

'He did and it's my turn to apologise for putting you to so much trouble.'

'It was no trouble. I had intended calling on Emma, but she was out too so I had time on my hands.'

Jack's face tightened at the mention of Emma's name and Sophie remembered he still thought she was a reporter.

'I'm not . . . ' she began.

'Me first, I think.' Jack held up a hand stopping her mid-flow. 'Then we'll be on our way.'

'We don't have to leave yet, Daddy, do we?' Harry piped up. 'It's nice here. I like being with Sophie. She's fun.'

'I'm sure she is, but she's a busy lady and we can't arrange our schedules to suit you.'

'Can I come again then, Sophie?'

'That's something you'll have to arrange with your father,' she evaded a direct answer.

'I hope it won't happen again,' Jack said. 'As soon as I got back I checked with the school. Harry was supposed to have given me a letter from his teacher about the training day, but I never received it.' He looked meaningfully at his young son.

'I got a lift to the lockup, Daddy, from one of the cleaning ladies. Bill wasn't in his box so I ran under the barrier. I was going to let myself in but I couldn't open your door. Then Sophie arrived and we had a nice time playing and things.'

'I shudder to think what might have

happened,' Jack lowered his voice in order not to alarm his son. 'I'm seriously in your debt.'

'I don't think Harry had been there very long before I arrived. Bill couldn't really take on the responsibility of keeping an eye on him, so I offered to bring him back here with me.'

'Thank you.' Jack cleared his throat uncomfortably. 'I realise I've been less than polite to you in the past,' he began.

'And I think it's time I put you straight on one or two things. Emma is an old school friend of mine,' Sophie replied. 'I'm not spying on her, nor am I trying to snap an indelicate photo of her.'

'Then what are you doing at the unit?' There was a trace of the old Jack in his brusque question.

'I can't tell you that,' Sophie replied.

'You can't blame me for getting the wrong idea. You had a tape recorder in your bag and several reporters have been sniffing around trying to get an exclusive.'

'Why?'

'That's something I can't tell you,' Jack replied.

'Would it be anything to do with Iain Buchanan?'

Jack's brown eyes reflected his surprise. 'So you do know about him?' The mistrust was back in his voice.

'I only recently found out about his relationship with Emma. He was with her the last time I called round and she introduced me.'

'Then you can understand why I thought you were up to no good. I've had several undercover reporters pretending to want their cars seen to. You'd be surprised at the excuses they come up with to try to get an interview.'

'Look, Mr West . . . '

'Jack, please.'

'Very well, Jack, if Emma wants you to know why I'm visiting her I'm sure she'll tell you, but it is of a private nature so can we leave it at that?'

'If you wish. I wouldn't want to pry into her private life.'

'Neither would I,' Sophie said firmly. 'She did say you would take any messages I had for her and that was why I came over to your unit the day we met in order to introduce myself, nothing else. I was waiting to turn into the unit on the day you caught me at the end of the drive in my car. Emma had just driven out in what I now know was Iain's car.'

'In that case I can only apologise again. Obviously I over reacted. Emma looks after Harry when my mother is busy, so in return I feel a sense of duty towards her.'

'Is that all you feel?' Sophie asked.

'I don't understand.' Jack frowned.

'I understand that you were once an item?'

'Hardly,' Jack smiled ruefully. 'We went out a couple of times together but there was nothing in it. The Emma Mountjoys of this world don't mix with humble car mechanics.'

The atmosphere in the kitchen was warm and relaxed. In the background

Sophie could hear Harry scribbling away at his picture and Bryony who had now fallen asleep in her basket was snoring gently.

'Do you fancy some chips?' Sophie asked looking down at the remains of their lunch, which had now gone cold.

'My son already seems to have eaten you out of house and home.'

'The chocolate cake was my mother's.'

'Mrs Sophie's chocolate cake is the best in the world, Daddy. Even nicer than Nanny's.'

'Don't let her hear you say that,' Jack warned his son, 'or you'll be in serious trouble.'

Harry giggled and used his finger to lick up the few crumbs of cake remaining on the plate.

'So, if you're not a reporter,' Jack asked the question Sophie had been dreading as she busied herself at the oven, 'am I allowed to ask what you do?'

She no longer wanted to score one

over on Jack West. Now she knew a little more about him, she could sympathise with his actions. Sophie had no love for some sections of the press either, but she had to keep in with them and she relied heavily on the resources of the local newspaper to help her with her research.

'I'm an enquiry agent,' she admitted.

'A what?' Jack frowned.

'A Ms Fix It, I suppose you could say.'

'And Emma's employed you?'

'Yes.'

★ ★ ★

There was a tempting smell of hot potatoes as Sophie opened the oven door and put more chips on the table.

'I think I'm going to have to go on a strict diet for the rest of the week,' she joked. 'This is my second portion of chips today and I've already scoffed a more than elegant amount of chocolate cake.'

'Perhaps you'd have dinner with me one evening?' Jack suggested, 'as a thank you for looking after Harry today?'

Sophie's warm chip dangled from her fingers.

'Can I come too?' Harry asked sneaking a chip off his father's plate.

'Manners,' Jack reprimanded his son, 'and no you can't.'

'Why not?'

'Because we'd like to go somewhere grown up and little boys have to be in bed by nine.'

'But, Daddy . . . '

'Come on.' Jack pushed away his empty plate. 'Miss Blaze has work to do and we are in danger of outstaying our welcome. Now what do you say to Miss Blaze?'

'I can call her Sophie, Daddy, I bet you can too. He can, can't he, Sophie?'

'If he wants to,' Sophie said with a slow smile.

Her eyes locked with Jack's. He was dressed in work stained clothes and there was the usual smell of oil on his shirt. His hair too needed a trim and he didn't look as though he'd had a chance to shave that morning.

'So, Sophie, you still haven't answered my question.'

'Sorry?' She dragged her attention back to the kitchen and began stacking their plates. It helped to have something to do with her hands.

'About dinner?'

'Say yes, Sophie,' Harry insisted, 'then you can come back to our house and tell me all about it. We can have some of Nan's chocolate cake and a glass of milk.'

'What girl could refuse an invitation like that?' Jack asked, his crooked smile threatening to dissolve the last vestiges of Sophie's reserve.

The two males continued to look expectantly at her while she hesitated over her answer.

She swallowed. She must remember her relationship with Jack was nothing more than providential. It would do no good making promises to a little boy just because his Daddy had eyes that would make an iceberg want to melt in one sitting.

'Why, um,' she cleared her throat carefully, 'why don't you call me some time? Perhaps we can fix something up?'

She hoped her reply sounded suitably casual.

'Yay.' Harry clearly took it as a yes. 'Can I take my drawing home too please, Sophie? I'd like to show it to Nanny.'

'Yes, of course.'

'Right.' Jack began gathering up his son's school bags. 'Come on then. Have you got everything?'

Bryony pattered out onto the landing with Harry giving Sophie an excuse to wave over the banister as they negotiated the stairs.

Back in her flat she sat down and tried to recover her senses. It was only a thank you dinner date she reminded herself sternly. It was important not to

114

read too much into the invitation.

She yanked her bag towards her and checked her mobile for messages. There was nothing as yet from Emma.

She began leafing through her case notes then frowned. A page was missing. Surely she hadn't dropped it?

One of Harry's coloured pencils rolled across the table towards her. Sophie picked it up and rolled it round in her fingers before the truth hit her like a punch in the stomach.

Harry had been drawing pictures of Bryony on the back of her notes and the sheet of paper missing was the one about her theory on Sir Gerald's purported relationship with Naomi Baxter.

Emma Calls Off
The Search

'I want you to drop the case,' Emma informed Sophie the next time they got together

'I don't understand.' Sophie frowned at her.

The chink of glasses and murmur of conversation around them made Sophie think that perhaps she had misheard Emma.

'It's perfectly clear, isn't it? I don't want you to go on with the investigation.'

'Why? Is it something to do with Jack?' she asked.

'Jack?' It was Emma's turn to look puzzled.

'He doesn't still think I'm spying on you does he?'

'I've no idea I haven't spoken to him.'

'Then why don't you want me to continue with my enquiries?'

Emma had insisted they sit in a discreet corner of the wine bar, one that wasn't overlooked by any of the other booths. She was also speaking in a low voice as if she were anxious not to be overheard.

The whole thing had left Sophie feeling completely baffled. Emma's text suggested they meet up on neutral territory, that they arrive separately and that Sophie was not to go anywhere near Emma's studio.

'I'm not sure I have to give a reason, do I?' Emma replied.

'No you don't, but I would like to know. All this secret texting is very cloak and dagger,' Sophie said. 'Have I done something wrong? Behaved unprofessionally? Is that it?'

'No, of course not.'

'Is it Iain then? I know I shouldn't have teased him, but I was only standing up for you.'

'It's nothing to do with Iain either. I

don't want you to go on with your enquiries for personal reasons.'

Emma's nervous body language was beginning to rub off on Sophie and she too began to glance over her shoulder to make sure no-one was hovering behind them or trying to eavesdrop on their conversation.

'You're going to have to do better than that,' Sophie insisted.

'If you must know,' Emma paused reluctantly, 'I've received a strange telephone call.'

'You're being threatened?' Sophie raised her eyebrows.

'No, nothing like that,' Emma assured her, 'at least I don't think it was a threat.' She bit her lip as if uncertain how to continue.

'What happened?' Sophie prompted Emma in frustration when she didn't speak. 'If someone's harassing you then I ought to know about it.'

'The nature of the telephone call suggested the story of my involvement with Iain is about to break.'

'Have you any idea who made the call?'

'None at all.'

'Was it a man or woman?'

'A woman, but don't you see, if what she said is true then I'll need to keep a low profile? The studio won't be best pleased if they learn I've been employing a private detective to delve into my past.'

Sophie pondered on Emma's explanation, still not totally convinced she was being honest with her.

'But why did you want us to meet up here? Surely it would have been less public to meet in your studio?'

'If someone from the press saw us together at my studio, they'd be bound to run a check on you.'

'Aren't they just as likely to see us together in a wine bar?' Sophie suggested, but Emma wasn't listening.

'Can you see the headlines? *Female 'Tec Delves Into Mountjoy's Past*? What does the delectable Emma have to hide?'

Sophie raised an eyebrow over Emma's colourful imagery.

'Not the sort of thing we want to read over the breakfast table, is it?'

'Aren't you getting a little carried away?' Sophie enquired with a wry smile.

'I don't think so.' Emma looked slightly affronted over Sophie's casual reaction to her fears. 'You don't seem to be taking the situation at all seriously.'

'Sorry, I didn't mean to be rude,' Sophie apologised, 'but I honestly don't think it is that serious.'

At the back of her mind, Sophie couldn't help suspecting that Emma was secretly enjoying herself. She had always been a bit of a drama queen and loved being the centre of attention. She often played the lead in the school play and Sophie began to wonder if she wasn't acting out a role now.

'Well, I do.'

Sophie began to feel sorry for Emma. Perhaps the call had spooked her. She wasn't looking her usual chic self. The extraordinary hat she had been wearing when she had scuttled into the wine bar had mussed up her hair and her clothes were a strange mixture of dress down shabby and grunge.

'I really can't afford to attract any adverse publicity and as I've already said if the tabloids discovered I'd employed an enquiry agent to delve into my past they'd have a field day trying to find out why.'

Emma ran a hand through her untidy hair. There were dark shadows under her eyes and Sophie suspected she hadn't had much sleep lately.

'Surely then it's vital I find out exactly what happened to Tony and Naomi Baxter,' Sophie insisted, 'that way if there is anything connecting their disappearance to your father, you'll be prepared.'

Sophie hadn't yet told Emma about her lost page of notes, but she had managed to leave a message on Jack's voicemail to ask for its return. Deciding not to worry Emma with that bit of news Sophie smiled brightly in an attempt to lift Emma's spirits.

'Whatever happened was over twenty years ago so I'm sure it won't create much of a scandal now.'

'Exactly, so we don't need to bother investigating it.'

Emma thrust out her chin in a stubborn gesture of defiance, one Sophie recognised from the past. When Emma was in one of these moods there was no budging her.

'Have you told Iain about the telephone call?' Sophie asked.

'Yes.'

'What does he think?'

'He's worried too. He thinks that the studio might accuse him of breaching the terms of his contract.'

'Surely the fact you received an anonymous telephone call is more important than the terms of his contract?'

'Iain doesn't think so.'

Again Sophie wasn't surprised. Iain Buchanan had struck her as a self-centred individual. She supposed it went with the territory when you were an actor.

'He doesn't want the news of our engagement jeopardising his chance of getting the film part he's been going after. His second audition went well and his agent says it's now between him and one other actor. So I really don't want to rock the boat. You do understand, don't you?'

Sophie's antipathy to Iain Buchanan was in danger of turning into deep dislike. What sort of man only thought of himself and his career when his future fiancée's happiness was at stake?

Emma smiled shakily. 'Thank you for all the trouble you've gone to,' she added as she sipped her wine. 'Have you got any other work on your books?' she asked politely.

'Things are a bit quiet at the moment,' Sophie admitted. 'I may take a little holiday. It's been a while since I've had a break.'

'Good idea. Iain and I had hoped to go to Amalfi for our honeymoon. I've always liked Italy. We wanted to visit my aunt at the same time. Iain's never met her.' Emma did her best to smile. 'But we've had to put our plans on hold for the time being.'

'Well I hope everything turns out all right for you.'

Sophie was beginning to run out of conversation. Without the case to discuss the two girls had very little common ground.

'I heard about your little adventure with Harry,' Emma changed the subject.

Sophie had been trying hard not to think about Jack. His invitation to dinner was obviously only a thank you for looking after his son and it was important that she didn't read too much into the gesture. All the same, it was difficult not to look forward to seeing him again. Jack West was different from every other man she had met. Most of Sophie's past boyfriends hadn't been able to cope with the erratic nature of her career and the relationships generally dwindled out of steam after a few dates.

'He showed me the drawing he'd made of Bryony.'

'Who Jack?' Sophie hoped no-one had read her notes on the back. 'I thought you hadn't seen him.'

'I haven't. Harry showed it to me. It was very, er, colourful, wasn't it? He wants his father to pin it up on the wall in the workshop. I think it's a form of subtle blackmail. Harry would love to have a dog and I suppose he thinks if Jack sees a picture of one every day it might work.'

Sophie's heartbeat thumped against her chest. Thank heavens Emma hadn't thought to turn the drawing over.

'When was this?' she asked casually.

'This afternoon. I was working in the studio so I was able to look after Harry while Jack did some business with a new customer. Because of all the disruption this morning he was running behind.'

Sophie knew she had to get that drawing back from Jack as soon as possible. It was far too dangerous a document to leave hanging up on a wall in a workshop.

'But Jack can be stubborn at times and I think Harry may have a battle on his hands about getting a dog. The owners of Stable Yard are strict about the no pets rule on the premises and I don't think Jack would feel safe having an animal so close to the river.'

'The river?' Sophie frowned.

'Jack's cottage overlooks the River Mole. It's a lovely little place, all nooks and crannies and oak beams. There's a sweet little garden that his mother tends to when she gets the chance. It's a bit remote for my taste but Jack loves it there. So does Harry.'

'It sounds a lovely place to bring up a child.'

Sophie tried to ignore the reluctant stab of jealousy she felt at the thought of Emma and Jack sharing intimate suppers in the garden of his riverside cottage.

She and her brothers had grown up

in a similar cottage. Even now the smell of wood smoke and autumn apples could evoke powerful memories.

Sophie's parents' cottage wasn't very big and space was cramped, but she and her brothers had loved the rickety staircase and the sloping wooden floors. When friends and family came to stay Sophie, Tom and Sam used to decamp into two tiny attic rooms under the eaves and frighten each other with ghost stories. She smiled at the memory.

'It was lucky you found him that morning, wasn't it?'

Emma's voice broke into her thoughts.

'Sorry?'

'Harry. He said he'd rung my bell but there was no reply.'

'I was actually intending to call on you as well with a case update,' Sophie explained.

'Hmm?' Emma began checking her mobile messages. 'Nothing from Iain. What was that about updates?'

'The reason why I called on you.'

'To update me on your progress with

Jack?' Emma teased.

'There is no me and Jack.' Sophie protested, wishing she didn't blush so easily.

A knowing smile softened Emma's lips. 'You were never very good at fibbing, were you? Even at school I could always tell when you were being economical with the truth.'

'I've no idea what you are talking about.' Sophie shifted uncomfortably in her seat.

'Go on, admit it. You like Jack.'

'Even if I did, which I don't. He doesn't like me.'

'You're perfect for each other. I think I might play cupid.'

'You'll do no such thing, and this conversation stops here and now,' Sophie said firmly.

'Sorry, didn't mean to tease.'

'Look,' Sophie cleared her throat and spoke carefully. 'I know you said you didn't want to go on with the investigation but what I wanted to tell you is that I do think your father knew Naomi Baxter.'

'It doesn't matter now. I told you I'm dispensing with your services.' Emma glanced at her watch then began rooting around in her bag. 'I'm going to have to go. Work is piling up and I need to do an all nighter. One or two outstanding commissions are getting rather urgent.' Her amber eyes danced with amusement. 'As a result of all these unofficial rumours about me and Iain my selling power has rocketed. People are beginning to clamour for an original Emma Mountjoy. They want them to hang on their wall to impress their friends. I've actually got a waiting list. Can you believe it?'

'Good for you,' Sophie congratulated her friend. If Emma didn't want to listen to what she had to tell her, then she couldn't force her. 'I hope it all turns out well for you.'

Emma held out her hand. 'I suppose this is goodbye?'

'I suppose it is,' Sophie agreed.

'Unless we bump into each other on the common again.'

'If we do, I'll try to keep Bryony out of your way,' Sophie promised.

'I'd better leave first if you don't mind,' Emma donned an enormous pair of dark glasses. 'I feel rather silly wearing these, but Iain has insisted.' She rammed her hat back onto her head. 'There, disguise complete. What do you think?'

'It's, um, very disguising,' was all Sophie could come up with as she looked at the strange ensemble.

Emma blew Sophie a kiss then with a final tug on the brim of her battered fedora she hurried out of the wine bar.

Sophie stayed where she was for a few moments more to think things through. Hopefully Jack would read her text message once he'd finished with his customer. She found the thought that she would no longer bump into him outside Emma's studio oddly depressing, but Emma no longer needed her services, so Sophie would have no reason to call round.

She would miss Harry too. The little

boy was good company and reminded her of her nephews. He seemed rather a solitary child and had Sophie got to know Jack better, she would have enjoyed introducing Harry to her nephews.

She tried to be upbeat about the lack of work on her books. Something was bound to turn up, but periods of inactivity made her feel restless. She disliked hanging around waiting for the telephone to ring. There was always paperwork to catch up on she supposed but that was something else she didn't really enjoy.

Her mobile phone vibrated with an incoming text.

Dinner tomorrow? she read Jack's message.

Sophie texted an acceptance and asked Jack to bring Harry's drawing with him, explaining about the notes on the back. She knew she could rely on Jack's integrity not to read them.

Sophie collected her things together and left the wine bar. The night air was fresh and Sophie took a few deep breaths to clear her head. A shadowed movement behind her caught her attention and she swung round.

'Was that Emma Mountjoy with you earlier?' A T-shirted man sidled up to her.

Sophie was instantly on her guard. Until then she had half suspected Emma of imaging that she was being followed.

'No comment,' she said as a flashbulb went off in her face, temporary blinding her. 'Hey, what do you think you're doing?' she demanded, outraged by the liberty. 'You have no right to take my photo.'

'You are Sophie Blaze, aren't you?' The reporter was scribbling furious notes onto a pad. 'Are you interested in an exclusive?'

'What?' Sophie lost her footing and stumbled. Her handbag slipped out of her fingers.

'Your friendship with Emma Mountjoy? What she was really like at school?'

'You've got the wrong person.'

The reporter pounced on one of her

business cards littering the pavement.

'Give that back.' Sophie tried to snatch it from him.

'Thought so,' he crowed. 'This tells me all I need to know. See you, Sophie and thanks for the exclusive.'

'I didn't give you one,' Sophie protested.

'Well, any time you're interested in doing a deal, let me know.'

Appalled at their behaviour Sophie tried to run after them to demand the return of her card, but they were already revving up a powerful motorbike that would easily out distance her and her car.

Impotent with a mixture of indignation and shock, Sophie fumed as she watched the bike turn the corner and disappear in a cloud of smoke.

How had they got onto her? She knew several of the local reporters, but these were not two she recognised.

If this was what Emma had to put up with, then Sophie understood her apprehension. She did not envy Emma's lifestyle one little bit. Emma. She frowned. Why hadn't they pursued Emma after she'd left the wine bar? Sophie hadn't liked to disillusion her friend, but a hat and a pair of chain store sunglasses would not be sufficient disguise to fool an experienced enquiry agent or a keen eyed reporter. It took hours of make up to do the job properly.

With her head still buzzing, Sophie unlocked her car. Her stomach was churning with unease as she jumped in and drove back to her flat.

'I'm A Private
Enquiry Agent'

'I am sorry about this,' Jack apologised as they sipped mugs of hot chocolate and listened to the soothing night sounds emanating from the river.

A cricket chirruped in the long grass and every so often there was a soft splash of something landing in the water. Sophie watched the ripples fan out then fade away.

'It doesn't matter,' she insisted.

'I called in several favours to book a table at short notice at the golf club for us. The range is floodlit at night and you get a spectacular view from the bay windows.'

'Honestly, I don't mind.'

'The food's better than beans on toast and a banana too.' There was a smile in Jack's voice. 'And small boys don't crawl all over the place demanding your attention.'

'There's no need to beat yourself up about it. Beans on toast is my absolute most favourite supper and I love crisps with orange juice as an aperitif.'

'I don't know how my mother came to get her dates muddled. She was supposed to babysit Harry. She said to apologise to you.'

'Mothers are entitled to a social life, you know,' Sophie insisted. 'Besides, I needed to apologise to Harry about snaffling his drawing and explain why I wanted it back.'

'Glad you did,' Jack said. 'He's been trying to persuade me to hang the thing up in the workshop. He's mad keen about getting a dog but it's not sensible this close to the river. I wouldn't be able to keep an eye on it and a small boy at the same time. One of them would be bound to wind up in difficulty.'

'Emma told me why you couldn't have a dog.' Sophie finished her chocolate and put the mug down on the terrace.

'When?'

'We had a drink together last night.' Sophie paused uncertain how much Jack knew about Emma's unsettling telephone call. 'We had a girls' night out.'

She would have liked to tell Jack about the incident with the two reporters outside afterwards as well but he had proved such a considerate host, she didn't want to spoil the atmosphere between them by mentioning the press. She still wasn't totally sure he believed her story about her relationship with Emma.

'Well with Harry tucked up safely in bed, we can get on with our evening. Hang on.'

Jack got up and disappeared for a few moments. Moments later the terrace was bathed in a rosy glow of light, followed by the gentle strains of a Mozart concerto.

'Like the atmosphere?' Jack reappeared carrying a tray.

'It's lovely.'

'Thought you might like some more refreshment. Only soft drinks as you're driving.'

Sophie indicated the terrace. 'Did you do the lighting yourself?'

'Yes. It took me a whole weekend. When I'm not at the lock up I like to keep busy. I can't really go out much as I need to be around for Harry. He's getting to an age where he needs a constant chauffeur on hand.'

The ghost of Harry's mother lingered on the night air between them.

'It can't be easy being a single parent,' Sophie spoke carefully having no wish to intrude on Jack's past personal life.

'There's my mother,' Jack said, 'and Emma's been wonderful.'

'You've known her a long time haven't you?'

'She was actually a friend of Linda's. That's how we met.'

Sophie knew of the glue binding Jack and Emma together. She remembered

Emma telling her they'd all met at a disco and despite Jack and Emma's mutual insistence that they were no more than good friends, Sophie suspected that wasn't entirely the case. The emotions they had shared as a threesome with Linda would always be a reminder of their past relationship.

'Emma is Harry's godmother,' Jack went on to say as he poured out two glasses of fruit juice.

That bit of news didn't surprise Sophie. What would be more natural than for Linda to choose one of her oldest friends for the honour?

'Here you are,' Jack passed over one of the fruit juices. 'Made to my mother's secret recipe,' he said.

'Are you an only child?' Sophie changed the subject.

'I'm one of seven actually,' Jack confessed.

'Seven?'

'Don't look so surprised. It does happen sometimes,' Jack's slightly off centre smile softened his face. 'I suppose growing up in a large family teaches you how to be self sufficient. If you don't fight your quarter, you don't survive. There was a lot of rough and tumble, but we're all actually good friends, although we don't meet up very often.'

'Where are they all now?'

'Three of my sisters live in Canada. The other one is in Scotland. My two brothers drop in from time to time. One's not married and the other is separated. He travels a lot and sort of lives out of a suitcase, so these days I often feel like an only child. Living so close to my mother I see the most of her, I suppose.'

A comfortable silence fell between them as they sipped their drinks.

'It's going to be a warm day tomorrow,' Jack predicted as he swatted a gnat.

'It's so restful here by the river, I'm surprised you ever want to leave it. Do you like water' Sophie asked.

Jack made a face.

'What's the matter?'

'I've a confession to make.'

Sophie looked at him expectantly. Jack eyed the crazy paving stones as if reluctant to look her in the eye then he gave a rather shamefaced smile.

'I can't actually swim. I used to bunk off lessons at school and go and make a nuisance of myself in the local garage.'

'You didn't?' Sophie laughed at this confession

'I was always crazy about all things mechanical and in those days there wasn't so much legislation about and as long as you were sensible, a young boy could crawl all over the shop and not get into too much trouble. That is until the headmaster found out about you. Then you were in for it. I can't count the number of hours I've sat outside his study quaking in my boots. Still it all came right in the end and like I say, I never did learn to swim.'

'What made you move down by the river then?'

'After my life changed,' he paused, 'Harry and I needed to move. The house we lived in was too big and held too many memories. When we first saw the cottage it was really run down and needed a lot doing to it but I was on a limited budget and the price was friendly because of the amount of renovation that would be involved to get it back in shape. It was only after we moved in that I remembered I wasn't a natural with water, but Harry loved it and so did I.'

The postage stamp of garden leading down from the patio was an abundance of bright flowers. There was a rickety crazy paving path weaving in and out of the lawn and Harry's swing creaked in a far corner as it swayed in the evening breeze.

Sophie leaned back contentedly. The cool breeze now fanned her face. She wondered how many other females, apart from herself and Emma, had enjoyed Jack's hospitality at Riverside Cottage. The music changed to a

Rossini overture, the choice perfectly suiting the garden setting.

Jack was a constant surprise to her. After their initial abrasive encounter when he had mistaken her for paparazzi, he had shown a considerate side to his nature that portrayed a more gentle and caring character.

He caught Sophie looking at the tooled leatherwork on the side of his boots.

'One of my sisters brought them over from Canada,' he explained. 'I wear them to disguise my limp, the result of dropping a jack on my foot many years ago. It damaged my toes and the injury still plays me up every now and then and I'm vain enough to want to disguise it.'

'The accident didn't put you off working with cars?'

'Not at all and it was my own fault. I wasn't paying attention to what I was doing. Not a mistake I shall make again,' he added, looking down at his jean clad legs. 'I know they are cowboy boots but I can't ride a horse either. Now you know all my guilty secrets.'

'I was never very sporty at school either. Emma was head of games and she used to drag me outside in horrible weather and make me run round the sports field.'

A look of alarm crossed Jack's face. 'That's a side to her character I've never seen. Hope she doesn't try it on me.'

'I think she's a lot more artistic these days.'

'And you're a Girl Friday aren't you?'

Sophie supposed as Emma was no longer her client, there was no harm in telling Jack what she really did for a living.

'Actually I'm a private enquiry agent.'

'A what?' he repeated in disbelief.

'I couldn't tell you earlier because Emma was a client, but last night she asked me not to continue with my investigations.'

Jack held up a hand to stall Sophie. 'Just a minute. Let me get this straight.

You're a detective?'

'Nothing so grand,' Sophie replied anxious to play down the more serious aspects of her work. 'I'm much more low key. I look into lost dogs, put families in touch with missing relatives, things like that.'

'And Emma's lost a dog?' Jack was now looking thoroughly confused. 'I didn't know she had one.'

'No,' Sophie hesitated. 'I can't really tell you what I was doing for her, it wouldn't be fair.'

'I suppose not,' Jack conceded. But I'm not working for the newspapers.'

Jack gave an embarrassed smile. 'Do I have to apologise for that mistake again?'

'Not necessary,' she assured him.

'Would I be right in guessing that this investigation you're not doing any more was something to do with Iain Buchanan?'

'Indirectly,' Sophie admitted.

What do you think of him?' Jack asked.

'I've only met him once,' Sophie hedged.

Jack grinned. 'Well I sort of wish Emma hadn't linked up with him. I've nothing personal against the man but the relationship is making life difficult for us on the industrial unit. Still, having said that, her personal life is absolutely none of my business.'

'Have you had many reporters nosing around your workshop?'

'Tell me about it. You remember that new customer I spent so much time on yesterday afternoon? The one with the rush job?' Sophie nodded. 'I went to answer the telephone leaving him alone in the workshop. When I came back I found him nosing around my private stuff.'

Sophie blinked nervously. She had a premonition that she wasn't going to like what was coming.

'I challenged him and he tried to pretend he was admiring Harry's drawing of Bryony. He fed me some story about his children liking dogs, but it wasn't very convincing.'

Sophie's beans on toast supper began to churn in her stomach.

'You didn't believe him?'

'No, but even if the story was true he had no business to go poking around the workshop. I knew from your text that you'd made some notes on the back so when I told him the drawing belonged to a friend of mine and was private he asked if the friend was Emma Mountjoy. Turns out he's a journalist and he wanted an exclusive from me.'

'What did you do?' Sophie hardly liked to ask the question.

'Well, the polite answer is I didn't bother finishing the work on his car. We had rather a heated exchange, but he couldn't object because I'd done most of the work and I didn't present him with the bill.'

'Did he have an earring and a pony tail?' Sophie asked, not really listening to Jack's reply.

The smile left his face, to be replaced

by a look of suspicion. His eyes narrowed as he looked at her.

'Yes.'

'I think I know him. He accosted me outside the wine bar last night.'

'What do you mean accosted you?'

'He must have seen Emma leave and he realised we'd been having a drink together. She was wearing a disguise but frankly it wouldn't have fooled a child. I thought she was going a bit over the top about being followed and didn't take her seriously. When I got outside he sort of pounced on me.'

'He didn't harm you?'

'No, but he took me by surprise. I dropped my bag and one of my business cards fell out. He jumped on it.'

'I hope that's all you had to do with him.'

The cool evening breeze now turned to a chill wind. Sophie sat up straight and tugged at her shawl.

'What made you think there was anything more?' she asked in a cold voice, all her earlier warmth towards

Jack vanishing in an instant.

'These reporters can talk eye watering figures for exclusives and now Emma no longer requires your services, it could be quite tempting to take up their offer.'

Sophie frowned at Jack, not wanting to misunderstand his meaning.

'If you're suggesting what I think you, are then let me tell you I have no intention of selling Emma's life story to the highest bidder.'

'I didn't mean that,' Jack began, but Sophie didn't give him a chance to interrupt.

'I do not go round touting tales about my friends to the newspapers. If I did, I'd have hardly any clients left. In my business you learn to be discreet. It's a shame it's not a requirement for car mechanics.'

'Now hold on a moment,' Jack tried to interrupt again, but Sophie wouldn't let him finish.

'Thank you for a lovely evening,' she managed to grind out. 'I think I'd better leave before I say something I might really regret.' She snatched up her bag and her car keys. 'Goodnight, Mr West.'

It was only as Sophie drove off that she realised she had left Harry's drawing and her notes on the table in Jack's dining room.

Emma Makes
Headline News

Sophie almost didn't answer the insistent ringing of her telephone. She was clutching a piece of toast and busy gaping at breakfast television. A huge picture of Iain Buchanan filled the screen. The sound was muted and by the time she had found the remote control and adjusted the volume the announcer had moved on to a new topic.

'Hello?' she snatched up the receiver, her voice breathless with annoyance over having missed the news item.

'Sophie, is that you, dear?'

'Who is this?' she asked warily.

'Mary Pritchard.'

Sophie frowned. The name was familiar but for the moment she couldn't place it.

'Berkham? Church Street Cottages?'

151

Mary prompted her memory. 'I put you in touch with Irene Bell, Mrs Crampton's daughter.'

'Sorry, yes, of course I remember you.'

'Did she contact you?'

'Irene? She did. Thank you.' Sophie decided there was no need to update Mary on subsequent developments. 'I'm sorry I didn't get back to you.'

'Actually, I've been doing a little sleuthing work of my own and I thought you might be interested in my findings.'

Sophie's heart sank. This was a complication she had not foreseen, but it was something that would be best nipped in the bud.

'I picked up quite a few interview techniques while I was typing up police reports.'

'That really won't be necessary, Mary,' Sophie did her best to stem the flow of her excited chatter. 'My investigations are complete and the case is now closed. Please don't concern yourself any more.'

'That's a pity,' Mary sounded disappointed. 'Could we meet up anyway?'

'What for?' Sophie asked before realising her remark had sounded rather rude.

'I've got a dentist appointment in Steepways this morning but I'm free afterwards. There's a new garden centre opened near you and I'd like to visit it if you fancy an afternoon out if you're not too busy? I'm looking for a new shed.'

As she drove to the garden centre Sophie wasn't too sure why she had accepted Mary's invitation. She had a backlog of paperwork to catch up on and she needed to deliver some new flyers advertising her services. Perhaps to make the exercise cost effective she could use her trip to the garden centre to promote them she thought as she drove into the car park. There was usually a notice board for such purposes in these places and she never travelled anywhere without a handy supply of pamphlets.

Mary had already arrived and was signalling frantically from behind a display of garden buildings.

Over soup and a bread roll Mary read from her capacious notes.

'You remember that rather dreadful bald-headed person who answered the door to cottage number three the day we met?'

'Yes,' Sophie replied carefully, hoping Mary hadn't done anything rash like trying to follow her example by speaking to the occupier.

'Well he knocked at my door the other day. He gave me such a fright I almost didn't open it. It seems he saw me talking to you. He thrust some boxes at me. Said he'd found them hidden away in the cottage. Goodness knows why the police didn't find them. Anyway I didn't detain him for too long.'

'Mary,' Sophie felt duty bound to offer a word of warning, 'you mustn't get involved any more.'

'I'm not really, dear. Things sort of involved me, didn't they? Where was I?

Oh yes. I didn't do anything about the papers immediately because my grandson wasn't well and what with one thing and another I was a bit tied up helping my daughter to look after him.' Mary adjusted her glasses, took another spoonful of her tomato soup then squinted at her notes. 'When I eventually got back home I spent an evening going through them and than I made a note of the relevant bits rather than bring all the papers with me. There were business letters, medical appointments, the sort of things I should imagine you don't bother to take with you should it be necessary to leave home in a hurry.'

'Mary,' Sophie did her best to stop her garrulous friend, 'the client has asked me to close my investigations.'

'I know, dear, you said, but I thought you ought to know that Tony and Naomi Baxter weren't married, they were brother and sister.'

'I know.'

'Did you also know that Tony resigned from his job with the Council just before they disappeared?'

'No, I didn't,' admitted Sophie.

'I found the letter and it would explain their sudden disappearance, wouldn't it?'

'Perhaps it would, but I expect the police went into it all at the time.'

'I wonder if they went abroad? It would have been more difficult to trace their whereabouts in those days. They could have changed their names as well I suppose.'

'Why?' Sophie was intrigued. Mary had opened up some new avenues of thought.

'Start a new life? I think Tony Baxter might have been a very controlling sort of person.'

'How do you know that?'

'A brother and sister living together with the sister's baby?'

'It's not that unusual.'

'Where was the baby's father?'

'I don't know.'

Mary had now finished her soup and was attacking the remains of her bread roll. 'Perhaps the father was married.'

'Or Naomi could have reverted to her

maiden name after a marriage that went wrong,' Sophie suggested. 'What could be more natural than for her brother to help her out?'

Mary mulled over this piece of news thoughtfully.

'You're right, I suppose. There are a number of explanations. No wonder the police were puzzled. Perhaps Tony simply wanted to make a new start.'

Sophie now began to have doubts that Emma's father was the father of Naomi's baby as there was no legal reason for them not to get married, but that didn't explain why he had kept their details hidden away among his private papers for so many years.

Mary passed over several pages of scribbled notes. 'Anyway, for what it's worth, the notes are yours. If you want the original paperwork it's at home.'

'Thank you.' Sophie slipped them into her bag, knowing she would probably never read them. Mary's take on the case was so full of holes it leaked.

'If you've finished your lunch do you

fancy a walk round?' Mary suggested. 'I've only got a tiny garden, but I nearly always find something to spend my money on in these places.'

'I need to visit the admin office actually on a business matter,' Sophie replied.

'In that case,' Mary looked at her watch, 'I'll see you back here in an hour? We can finish off with a cup of tea and a gooey cake?'

Sensing Mary was at heart a bit lonely and not wanting to spoil her day out, Sophie agreed. Carefully re-applying her lipstick and dabbing a suggestion of blue-bell eau de toilette on her wrists, Sophie headed for the office.

She was pleased to see the manager of the garden centre was male. It was easier to turn on the charm. Being slender and blonde often had its advantages and Sophie decided to use her natural assets to best effect.

'It's not the sort of service our customers would need,' the manager explained after he'd browsed through Sophie's pamphlets. 'They might get the wrong idea. I mean why would our patrons need to employ an enquiry agent? It suggests unwholesome activities in the area.'

'I expect a lot of them have got dogs,' Sophie's face was beginning to ache with the pressure of smiling so hard. 'And dogs go astray. When they do they need to be traced. Cats have a habit of disappearing too. Have you got any animals?'

'As a matter of fact I have.'

'How would your children feel if one of their pets disappeared?'

'Devastated,' the manager admitted.

'They would be doubly devastated if you did nothing about it wouldn't they?' Sophie pushed home her advantage. 'My charges are very reasonable.' She lowered her voice hoping the manager would lean forward to better hear what she was saying. Older men she knew liked the smell of bluebells. Sophie raised her hand and pretended to pat down her hair. 'I'm discreet, local and I have a high success rate.'

A rueful smile softened the manager's

lips. 'Have you tried selling ice to Eski-mos?' he asked, 'because if you haven't, I think you'd be a roaring success.'

'Then you'll take some pamphlets?' A delighted Sophie handed over a fat bundle tied up with a rubber band.

'I can't display them on the front desk.' After looking at them the man-ager appeared to have second thoughts.

'Perhaps the staff would be interested?'

'I'll see. Thank you,' he glanced down at the pamphlets again, 'Miss Blaze.'

They shook hands.

Outside again in the fresh air, Sophie took a deep breath. Flushed with what she hoped was the success of her enquiry she didn't immediately notice a man walking towards her and cannoned into the hard wall of his chest.

'Sorry,' she gasped, her eyes watering from the impact.

'Are you all right?'

Sophie blinked. She would have recognised the voice anywhere.

'What are you doing here?' she de-manded.

'I could ask you the same question,' Jack replied.

'I was having lunch with a friend if you must know.'

'In the manager's office?'

'That was business.'

'Don't tell me he needs your professional services?'

'If you'll excuse me,' Sophie tried to side step away from Jack. He put out a hand to detain her. 'I'm due to meet someone in the snack bar.'

'Don't go. I've still got your notes. You left them on the table last night when you rushed out. Look, I'm sorry. I realise what I said came out badly.'

Sophie tossed back her hair. 'No, it came out correctly. I don't have any work on hand and if you must know I was trying to persuade the manager here to display my pamphlets.'

'I see. Well I'm returning his car. He wanted some work done on it.'

'Fine, well in case you are still harbouring doubts about my character let me make one thing clear.'

Jack's brown eyes narrowed. 'Now what are you talking about?' he demanded looking confused.

'I'm referring to Emma's relationship with Iain Buchanan.'

'Yes?' A wary expression crossed Jack's face.

'Let me assure you once and for all the press won't find out about it from me. I may be touting for business but I'm not that desperate.'

'So it wasn't you who leaked the story to the national news?'

'There you are, Sophie.' Mary appeared from behind another garden shed, clutching more brochures. 'I must say this place is a den of temptation. I've given my details to at least half a dozen salesmen. They are all such handsome young men and very persuasive.' She glanced at Jack. 'I'm sorry, dear. I didn't mean to interrupt your conversation with your friend. I'll wait for you in the snack bar.'

'No need, Mary. I'm just coming.'

'Mary Pritchard.' She beamed at Jack. 'I'm helping Sophie with one of her investigations.'

'Pleased to meet you.' Jack smiled politely. 'You don't look like a gumshoe to me.'

Mary laughed and Sophie could see she was completely bewitched by Jack's inherent good manners.

'I'm not really. In fact I'm a bit of a nosy old woman, but it's nice to feel wanted occasionally, isn't it?'

'Indeed it is.'

'I'll order two coffees and cakes, shall I, Sophie? Would you care to join us, Mr . . . ?'

'Jack West. Another time perhaps? I have to get back to collect my son from school.'

'In that case you can tell me about him another time.' Mary beamed at him. 'I have a little grandson. I've got a photo somewhere.' She began rummaging in her capacious handbag. Sophie's eyes met Jack's amused ones over Mary's bent head.

'Sorry,' she mouthed at him.

'Here it is.' Mary produced a school

photo of a smiling little boy. 'Bobby is six. How old is your son?'

'Five.'

Mary nodded. 'A lovely age isn't it?'

'It is indeed.'

'Well, see you in a minute, Sophie.' She bustled away.

'Thank you,' she said.

'What for?'

'Not being rude to her.'

'Why did you think I would?' Jack looked surprised.

'Because of me?'

'That's about as daft as my suggesting you would shop Emma to the newspapers because you haven't got any work on. I was only trying to warn you of the tricks newspaper reporters would resort to, nothing more.'

'What were you saying about a leaked story before Mary interrupted us?'

'You didn't see it on the news?'

'I did see a picture of Iain on breakfast television but I had the sound turned down, then Mary telephoned and by the time we'd finished the call the news was over.'

'The story about their relationship has broken. It's headline news. That's why I'm here. I had to get away. The industrial unit is crawling with reporters. Bill is having a tough time keeping them out.'

'What about Emma? You haven't deserted her?' Sophie demanded.

'I haven't seen her today. She rang through to say she needed to keep her telephone line clear for urgent calls, so I abandoned ship.'

Sophie bit her lip. 'If she wants some company tell her to give me a ring.'

'Would you like me to drop your case notes over to her when I've a spare moment? I could see how she is and pass on your message?'

'Er,' Sophie hesitated. Jack's suggestion put her on the spot. She wasn't sure she wanted Emma to read her notes before she had a chance to explain her reasoning behind them.

Before she could reply the garden centre manager emerged from his office.

'I'd better go,' Jack waved at him. 'Keep in touch.'

With her head in a whirl Sophie made her way to the snack bar.

'What a shame your gentleman friend is married,' Mary said as Sophie settled down to her coffee.

'He's actually a single parent,' Sophie replied then wished she hadn't.

'In that case, dear,' Mary responded with an arch smile taking in Sophie's heightened colour, 'I would suggest you don't let the grass grow under your feet. Indeed if I were a few years younger, I'd give you a run for your money.'

'Mary,' Sophie reproached her, 'there is nothing of that nature between Jack West and myself, nor are we remotely attracted to each other.'

Sophie was beginning to find everyone's views on her supposed relationship with Jack a tad tedious.

'Of course not, dear,' Mary responded with a knowing smile, 'now will you have the éclair or the cream slice?'

'They Were My Private Notes'

The following few days were a night-mare of press intrusion. Anyone who had anything to do with Emma Mountjoy was door-stepped by the media and the tabloids were full of the engagement news and speculation about Emma and Iain's wedding details.

Sophie had hoped to keep a low profile and that no-one would connect her with Emma, but the pony-tailed reporter who had accosted her outside the wine bar on the night she and Emma had shared a drink together was onto her case.

'How did you find out where I live?' Sophie demanded as she jogged back to her flat one morning to find him prowling around on the pavement outside.

'I got your details off your business card.'

'It doesn't give my private address.'

'It's amazing what you can find out when you tap a few details into a computer.'

She glanced over her shoulder. She didn't want to be caught standing on the pavement talking to a disreputable reporter, but she was equally reluctant to enter her flat. The reporter looked the type of person who would barge his way into the building behind her and she didn't fancy being in an enclosed space with him.

'You and Emma?' He persisted. 'She's the hottest news story around at the moment. Have you given any more thoughts to my offer of an exclusive?'

'I haven't changed my mind,' Sophie replied in a firm voice. 'The answer is still no. Now would you leave me in peace?'

'That's a pity.' The reporter feigned a regretful look. 'I could do you a very good deal.'

'I don't want one.'

'*My early years at school with Emma?*' he suggested. 'How we were friends, or enemies if you like? I've heard you and she had a few girlish differences?'

Sophie began to feel alarmed. This reporter whoever he was, seemed to have delved deeply into her personal background.

'There must be a new angle we can approach.'

'There isn't,' Sophie insisted, 'and if you don't stop pestering me I shall call the police.'

'But you are the police, aren't you?'

'No, I'm not,' Sophie retaliated.

The reporter glanced at the business card stapled to his note pad.

'My mistake.' he smiled. 'You're a private enquiry agent, aren't you? Tell me, did Emma consult you on a professional basis? Is there something in her past she would rather no-one knew about? An old family scandal perhaps?'

'Will you please leave me alone?'

Sensing her mistress's unease Bryony growled at the man.

'No need to lose your cool. I'm only doing my job. So you and Emma go way back?' He didn't wait for her reply. 'You bumped into each other by accident one day perhaps? What would be more natural than for old friends to catch up on old times? Emma discovered you were a private investigator and asked for your help? How am I doing?'

'I really don't have to listen to any more of this.'

'What exactly is your relationship with Jack West?'

The swift change of subject caught Sophie off guard.

'Steady.' The reporter put out an arm to steady her. 'We don't want you having an accident, do we?'

'I have no relationship with Mr West.'

'Then why is there a drawing of your dog pinned up on the wall of his workshop?'

The reporter was no longer smiling.

His narrow eyes and pointed nose reminded Sophie of a weasel. She was well used to handling herself in tricky situations, but then she reminded herself sharply, so was this man.

'It was you who wormed your way into his garage, wasn't it?' Sophie had great difficulty keeping her voice steady now. She could feel the situation was spiralling out of her control.

'I availed myself of Mr West's professional services, yes. No harm in that is there?'

'There is when you start prying through his private papers.'

'Correct me if I'm wrong, but people don't normally pin their private papers up in full view for anyone to take a look at, do they?'

'I have nothing further to say to you,' Sophie turned away from him.

In the distance she spotted her downstairs neighbour trundling up the hill with her shopping trolley. With a bit of luck, the reporter wouldn't push an elderly lady out of the way, in order to gain access to the block of flats.

'Well, if you change your mind, here's my number.'

'I won't.' Sophie didn't bother to take his card. 'Do you need some help, Mrs Atkins?' she smiled at her neighbour who had paused to catch her breath.

By the time Sophie had organised the trolley and helped Mrs Atkins with her shopping, the reporter had disappeared. Sophie decided to follow Emma's example and maintain a low profile. She would spend the rest of the day indoors catching up on her growing mountain of paperwork and updating her website which was in desperate need of a makeover.

The story was still hot news and although Sophie wasn't one for celebrity gossip she found it impossible not to catch each news bulletin as it was issued. There appeared to be no part of Emma's life that was untouched. Sophie recognised a picture of their old school and one of their teachers was interviewed. She gave a glowing report of Emma's prowess on the sports field and the number of cups she had won.

'Hello, dear.' Sophie's mother rang that evening. 'I suppose you've seen the news?'

'Do you mind if we don't talk about it, Mum?' Sophie replied in a weary voice.

'I understand, dear, but I was right, wasn't I? Emma Mountjoy was your old school friend?'

'Yes, she was.' Sophie switched off the television unable to face another inaccurate in depth biography.

'I do hope they don't get on to that uncle of hers.'

'What was that?' Until then Sophie had only been half listening to her mother.

'Roger Mountjoy. You remember him, he used to run a garage on the outskirts of town?'

'Did he have something to hide?'

'He was a bit of a ladies' man in his day. He cut rather a dashing figure, I seem to remember.'

'Did you know him?'

'Goodness me, no. We couldn't afford the likes of Roger Mountjoy's fees. Your father always serviced our cars himself. You used to help him, don't you remember? It was funny how Sam and Tom were never interested, isn't it?' Sophie listened as her mother chattered on. 'I don't know that I ever saw Roger Mountjoy. I saw Sir Gerald in the distance once or twice at your school events and I believe I might have been introduced to Emma's aunt, Roger's wife. She always seemed a rather sad woman to me, but we didn't really move in the same social circles.'

Neither did Naomi Baxter, thought Sophie. From the blurred images Sophie had seen of her, she seemed more homely than glamorous.

After a few more moments chatting to her mother and catching up on the family news and promising to visit her parents as soon as she could, Sophie put down the receiver. Although it hadn't been a physical day, she felt as exhausted as if she'd mounted a twenty-four hour surveillance operation.

★　★　★

Sun was streaming through the open window when Sophie woke up. She usually slept in on a Saturday and hadn't set the alarm the night before, so why was the bell ringing? In the few moments before full consciousness kicked in she realised it wasn't her alarm. Someone was vigorously attacking her front door bell. Bryony began barking and running towards the door, swept her tail from side to side in a gesture of welcome. Her reactions quelled Sophie's anxiety that it might be the intrusive reporter who had managed to gain access to the flats.

'Who's there?' she grabbed up her dressing gown and shrugged it on before padding along the corridor.

'It's me.'

'Jack? What are you doing here?'

The door was still on the security

chain and not wanting to be seen in her nightwear, Sophie poked her head round the gap.

'Quiet, Bryony, you'll wake Mrs Atkins with all that barking.'

'Here.' Jack thrust Harry's drawing through. 'I've brought back your notes.'

'Thank you very much.' Sophie ran a hand through her tousled hair. 'I'm sorry,' she stifled a yawn. 'I'm not respectable. I was asleep. Did you have to attack my bell so enthusiastically? What time is it?'

Her smile was met with a stony glare.

'What's wrong?' she demanded easing the crack in the door open a little wider.

'Those notes on the back of the drawing?'

Sophie turned them over. 'You've read them?' she asked, unable to believe what she was hearing. Until then she would have thought Jack's integrity was above snooping into private documents.

'You've done a very comprehensive job, haven't you?'

Sophie tossed back her head. She

wasn't sure of Jack's agenda but she resented the accusation that yet again she had done something wrong.

'They were confidential notes on a private matter and you had no right to read them. Correct me if I'm wrong, but weren't you going to give them back to Emma so she could read them in private?'

'There was no need. I should think half the country's read them by now.'

'What?' Sophie jolted upright.

'Read it for yourself. It's all here, word for word.'

A newspaper was thrust at her through the gap in the door. Under the headlines and a grainy photograph of Sir Gerald Mountjoy there was a picture of Naomi Baxter. Sophie didn't need to read the article. She could guess what it contained. She could also guess who was responsible for the story — the weasel-eyed reporter.

'I don't know anything about this,' Sophie insisted.

'You don't deny you wrote the report?'

'They were my private notes and they went astray while they were in your possession. Weren't you the one who left that reporter alone in your workshop?'

'So you do know what I'm talking about?'

Sophie was glad she hadn't fully opened her door. The expression on Jack's face was uncompromising. She thrust out her jaw, fed up with playing the victim.

'All I know is someone has used my notes without my permission.'

'They're pretty damning, aren't they?'

'They were also confidential.'

Sophie was aware she was breathing heavily and that her face was hot. What right did Jack West have to accuse her of anything? He was equally to blame for what had happened.

'Has Emma seen this?' Sophie asked in a softer voice.

'I spoke to her this morning,' Jack replied. 'She told me you were never really friends at school. She said you resented her popularity and that she wasn't surprised something like this happened.'

'You can't think this is some sort of revenge?' Sophie gasped.

'I don't know what to think, but she's very upset.'

'I'll telephone her later and explain.'

Sophie ran her eyes down the article. The contents were attributed to a source close to Miss Mountjoy. Sophie's name wasn't mentioned but Emma would know who was responsible.

'You won't be able to get in touch with her. She's gone away for a short holiday and she's keeping the destination a secret.'

'What about Iain?' Sophie asked. 'Has he gone with her?'

'They are no longer an item.'

'What?'

'The engagement has been broken off.'

'Broken off?' Sophie repeated in a daze.

'According to Emma, the studio is in talks about whether or not Iain has breached the terms of his contract.'

'Iain hasn't done anything wrong.'

'By associating with Emma he has.'

'Look, give me five minutes to get dressed. We need to talk things through.'

'I'm not staying.' Jack backed off. 'I've promised to take Harry and my mother down to the coast for the day.'

Sophie blinked myopically at him. It was in times of stress she often experienced colour confusion. Jack's shirt seemed to be a faded grey. Her vision blurred as she tried to concentrate on what he had just said.

'A day by the sea sounds lovely,' she tried to defuse the atmosphere between them. 'Am I invited too?'

'Family only,' was Jack's terse reply.

'Then why are you here?' Sophie demanded. 'Surely the return of my notes could have waited? Or did you want to accuse me of stirring up more trouble?'

'I've a message for you from Emma. She doesn't want to see you at Stable Yard again.'

'If those are Miss Mountjoy's wishes then she can tell me herself. She doesn't have to send you as a messenger boy and,' Sophie held up a hand before Jack could interrupt, 'I don't think Miss Mountjoy actually owns Stable Yard, does she?'

'You know she doesn't.'

'I thought not. So if I do have cause to visit the area neither you nor Emma has the power to stop me from doing so. I shall of course do my best to stay out of your way, because the wish not to meet up with you again is entirely mutual.'

'There's no need to shout. I'm not deaf.'

'There doesn't seem to be any other way of getting through to you.'

The answering flare in Jack's eyes convinced Sophie her barb had found its target.

'You should be pleased, all this fuss has done you a favour.'

'What sort of favour?' Jack demanded.

'Emma is footloose and fancy free again.'

'So?'

'You are in love with her, aren't you? I should imagine she would find yours is a very accommodating shoulder to cry on.'

'You don't know what you are talking about.'

'Don't I? You were the one who allowed my notes to fall into the hands of an unscrupulous reporter. I'm not so certain you didn't engineer the whole thing yourself. It's certainly very convenient to place the blame on me, isn't it?'

'That's a ridiculous suggestion.'

'Is it? It makes perfect sense to me, but we're going round in circles aren't we?'

It cost Sophie every inch of willpower to keep smiling at Jack. She was slow to anger but she knew if she stood talking to him through the crack in her door much longer, she would be in danger of saying something she really regretted.

'Don't let me keep you from your day out at the seaside. Give my love to Harry. I'm sorry I won't be seeing him again. He could give his father a few lessons in manners.'

Before Jack could reply and before her face crumpled, Sophie closed the door softly in his face. Trembling with barely suppressed anger she made her way into the kitchen. As she looked out of the balcony window she caught sight of Jack's van driving off. Yet again the prospect of never seeing him again was causing her an illogical amount of pain in the region of her chest.

She screwed up the newspaper report she was still clutching and threw it in the bin. In a gesture of defiance she raided the kitchen drawer and finding some adhesive, she taped Harry's picture of Bryony to the cupboard door. Her throat locked as she read the inscription in the corner. Harry had signed his drawing with his name and added the words, *This Is Bryony, Sophie's Dog and I Love Them Both.*

A Panic Over Harry

Bryony barked at Sophie's feet as she pounded through the long grass. Sophie took no notice. She needed to feel her muscles ache. She needed her chest to hurt when she tried to breathe. That was the only way she could deal with all that had happened recently in her life.

Emma was no longer speaking to her and Jack was blaming her for the break up of Emma's engagement. The only person on her side would seem to be Mary Pritchard.

'I only realised what it was all about when I read the newspapers, dear,' she explained down the telephone.

Sophie had been surprised and touched to receive her call.

'I didn't leak the story to the press.'

'I didn't for one moment think you did, dear.' Mary sounded shocked. 'Nor do I believe any of that nonsense about

Sir Gerald Mountjoy and Naomi Baxter. It's absurd. Besides which whatever he got up to in his private life was no-one's business but his own. His poor daughter must be distraught. These reporters want a taste of their own medicine is all I can say. I'm sure most of them lead very unsavoury lives. Anyway, dear, another reason I rang is because a very nice young man came and delivered my new shed yesterday. It's rather a grand affair I must say. It's even got power points installed so all I want to say is if life gets too dire for you in Steepways, there's always a bed here for you here, in the cottage of course. I'm not suggesting you sleep in the shed, nice as it is.' Mary laughed. 'I'm thinking of going the whole hog and creating a little patio area in front of it.'

'Thank you, Mary.' Sophie was touched by her offer. 'Things aren't quite that bad yet, but I may take you up on your offer.'

'You'll be most welcome. Come any time you like. How's that nice young man of yours? Jack was his name, wasn't it?'

Sophie was glad Mary couldn't see the expression on her face as she said, 'I haven't seen much of him recently now I'm no longer on the case. He was Emma's friend really.'

'Well, don't forget to drop in. No need to call first. I'm nearly always here.'

However hard she tried, she couldn't help thinking about Jack West. The only reason he was being so protective of Emma had to be because he was in love with her, despite his protestations. Why else was he so concerned about her and blaming Sophie for what happened?

It was almost as if he was looking for excuses to dislike her, but why?

The pain at the back of her calf muscles was now excruciating and drew Sophie up short. Even Bryony was beginning to look weary.

'Sorry, Bry,' she stroked her silky fur. 'Have I overdone it?'

Bryony licked her leg in a comforting gesture of support.

'Let's go back.' Sophie glanced at her watch and was surprised to see they had been out for over two hours.

By the time Sophie had attended to Bryony's damp paws and they'd both had a refreshing drink in the car, it was getting on for lunchtime. They hit Steepways at its busiest. Traffic in the centre of town was at a standstill. Sophie had forgotten it was market day, and the square was a jostling mass of confusion as stallholders unloaded their produce from their vans and bargain-hunting shoppers weaved in and out of the traffic. Vendors shouted out their wares at the top of their voices.

Sophie wound down her window and peered out.

'Mind your head, love,' a deliveryman cautioned her, 'if you don't want to be brained by a cabbage.'

She tapped her steering wheel in frustration. The drive home from the common usually only took ten minutes. Today it had already taken over half an hour and she still wasn't home.

'What's going on?' she asked one of the market stallholders.

In the distance she could hear the impatient hooting of car horns as tempers began to rise.

'Van's broken down up front,' he advised Sophie with a cheerful smile. 'It's blocked the road so no-one's going anywhere for a while.'

Sophie manoeuvred her hatchback into a quiet corner of the courtyard. She needed to stock up on provisions and it would save another journey.

'Want to stay there, Bry?'

She looked round to the back of the car. Bryony was stretched out on her rug behind the grill, her eyelids drooping from all the morning's activity. She began to snore.

Making sure the gap at the top of the window was open wide enough to admit some fresh air, Sophie grabbed up her shopping bag and headed back towards the market stalls.

The smell of fruit, mingled with those of cheese, fresh fish, flowers and

Mediterranean soaps. Most of the stallholders recognising Sophie as a regular, greeted her by name.

'Sophie, you're looking lovelier than ever.' Mick gave her a saucy wink as he popped a seeded batch loaf into one of his brown bags.

Sophie staggered back to her car, her shopping bag bulging with all her purchases. As she opened the door, she felt a rough hand shake her shoulder.

She spun round and stifled a shriek.

Jack was standing behind her, his eyes wild and his hair uncombed.

'Have you seen him?' he demanded.

'Who?'

'Have you seen Harry?'

'No. Should I have done?'

'He's disappeared.'

'What?' Sophie's shopping bag slipped to the ground. 'When?'

'You know how mad keen he is to have a dog and how he loves playing with Bryony? When I saw your car I thought perhaps he was with you.'

'Jack,' Sophie put her hand on his

arm. 'Tell me what's happened.'

'I'm trying to.'

'You're not making sense.'

'There was another training day at school.'

'Go on,' Sophie urged, longing to shake the story out of Jack. The thought of anything happening to Harry was almost more than she could bear.

'All the details were on the original letter, the one that Harry lost last time they had a training day, so I didn't know about it.'

'You mean they left him alone at Stable Yard again?'

'No. The cleaning lady delivered him safely to my unit just as an emergency call out came through. A van's broken down in the market.'

'Yes, I know.'

'I brought Harry along with me. I knew he would be safe here. I told him to stay in the van but when I looked for him he was gone. I've asked around but no-one's seen him.'

'He can't have gone far,' Sophie insisted.

'He's not at any of the stalls.'

'He hasn't been over this way. I would have seen him.'

'Where's Bryony?' Jack asked.

'We went out for a run and she was exhausted. She's snoozing in the boot.'

'No she's not.'

'She has to be.' Sophie pushed Jack out of the way and peered through the rear window. The boot was empty. Flinging open the hatchback Sophie snatched up Bryony's rug and held it to her face.

'It's still warm. She can't have been gone for long. Would Harry recognise my car and know how to open the boot?'

'All five-year-old boys know about cars and Harry would know how to open boot a lid. He's seen me do it enough times. Didn't you lock your car?'

'Let's not argue about that now. Where do you think they could have gone?'

'The Mole.' Jack ran a hand through his hair.

'What?'

'Harry loves walking by the river. He might have taken Bryony down there.'

'We'll keep on looking round the market,' Mick, the stallholder, rushed over to them as word got round that Jack's son was missing. 'Don't worry. We'll find the little lad. Ally, my wife, is organising a search party now.'

'Jack and I are going down to the river. Bryony is missing too. We think Harry might have taken her for a walk,' Sophie explained. 'You go that way,' she ordered Jack, 'I'll go the other.'

'Harry,' she called out as she ran towards the recreation ground.

The sun was scorching her back. With her heart in her mouth Sophie peered into every ditch and hedge, praying she would see Harry smiling back at her or hear Bryony's bark. There was nothing.

The air was cool and fresh down by the river. She looked up and down the deserted towpath. Bryony was a sociable dog and loved being the centre of attention. Somebody would have remembered if they'd seen her, but there was no sign of her or Harry.

If it hadn't been Harry who'd opened the boot, who had? There was no way Bryony could have undone the lock and let herself out. Besides she had been almost asleep when Sophie had gone off to do her market shopping.

In the distance she caught sight of a familiar figure jogging towards her from the far end of the towpath.

'Any luck?' Jack gasped.

'None.' Sophie shook her head. 'We're going to have to call the police.'

'I've been up and down the far stretch of the river three times and no-one's seen a thing. He's not in the market yard either.'

'Where was he when you last saw him?' Sophie demanded.

'I'm not sure. There were people everywhere and tempers were running high because the van was blocking the road. One man was a bit unpleasant and we had words. When I went back to my van to check on Harry he had disappeared.'

'We'll find him,' Sophie put a hand out to reassure Jack. The next moment they were seeking solace in each other's arms. Sophie rested her head on Jack's shoulder as he bent forward, burying his face in her hair.

'There's something I haven't told you,' he murmured.

'What?' Sophie raised her eyes.

'Harry heard us arguing last Saturday morning,' Jack confessed. 'He'd crept out the van. He wanted to ask you to come down to the coast for the day with us. Mrs Atkins was on her way out so she let him into the building. I found him crouching on the stairs. Because we were shouting he heard every word we said. He was heartbroken at the thought of not seeing you again.'

'Oh no.' Sophie stared at Jack aghast as all the bitter words she had hurled at him came back to haunt her.

'My mother did her best to console Harry with chips and ice cream on the seafront but nothing worked.'

'I'm so sorry. I shouldn't have said what I did.'

'You had every right to have a go at

me. I don't seem able to think straight where Emma's concerned. It's always been like that. She was my rock when I lost Linda.'

'Do you think Harry's gone to find Emma?' Sophie asked.

'He doesn't know where she is and even if he did he wouldn't go to her.'

'Why not?'

'He likes Emma but he's not allowed to touch things in her studio. Once or twice he's knocked things over and there's been a bit of a scene. He's far more likely to come looking for you. You get down and dirty when you're playing with him. He's always telling me how much he loves you.'

Jack's words made bittersweet listening and tore at Sophie's heart. Reluctantly she withdrew from the comforting circle of his arms.

'We have to find them,' she said in a voice barely above a whisper.

'You don't think one of them could have fallen in the water?' Jack asked.

'This stretch of the river isn't very

deep. I think they could clamber out.'

Sophie's mobile phone vibrated in her pocket. She snatched it out.

'Yes?' she gasped.

'Ms Blaze?' a male voice enquired.

'Who is this?'

'Mr Pollard. I'm the manager at the garden centre. You remember we met the other day and you left your leaflets with me?'

'I'm sorry, Mr Pollard, I can't talk now. I'll call you back.'

'No, don't. It was you talking to one of my rambling companions earlier at the river, wasn't it? Something about a little boy and a dog?'

'Yes.' Sophie was clutching her phone so hard, it was digging into the palm of her hand.

'Good news. They were asleep on the back seat of our bus. We found them after our coffee break.'

Sophie let out a shriek of joy then watched in dismay as her mobile phone slipped out of her hand and plopped into the water.

'The ramblers,' she shouted at Jack, not caring how many mobile phones she lost, 'they've found them in their bus. Jack, they're safe, both of them.'

Sophie had no idea what happened, but moments later she was kissing Jack. The touch of his lips on hers was setting her pulses on fire and all she knew was she didn't want him to stop.

Still No Sign Of Emma

'We finally made it,' Jack smiled at Sophie. 'A dinner date, without dogs, small boys or a telephoto lens pointed in our direction.' He leaned back in his padded seat.

Ever since Jack had kissed her down by the river, Sophie had had great difficulty sorting out where her emotions were going. She had never felt like this before. Jack had shown no regret over his impulsive action when they'd finally torn themselves apart and after he'd been reunited with a repentant Harry, she'd done her best to convince herself it had been no more than a spontaneous gesture of relief.

'What do you think of the view?' Jack asked.

'Stunning,' Sophie replied, still not quite believing the date with Jack West had actually materialised.

The view over the golf course was breathtaking. The large bay windows were open to let in the evening air. It was gone nine o'clock but one or two diehards were still playing on the floodlit range.

'They're keen,' Sophie said. 'Do you play?'

She realised she actually knew very little about Jack West, apart from the fact he ran a garage, was one of seven children and father to a five-year-old son.

'I don't really have the time. I'm a social member here, but I don't have much time to socialise either,' Jack admitted. 'My mother bought me my membership as a present. She thinks I should get out more.'

'You are sure your mother didn't mind having Harry tonight?'

'She loves having him, but I've told my son he's got to behave as he's still in disgrace for disobeying orders.'

'Don't be too hard on him,' Sophie pleaded. 'He was only doing what little boys do.'

'Disobeying their fathers?' Jack raised an eyebrow.

'Exploring. The market is full of lots of exciting things and when he saw my car with Bryony asleep in the back the temptation to take her for a walk proved too much.'

'Stop making excuses for him. You don't know the workings of a small boy's mind.'

'I've got some idea. I have three nephews and they are up to every trick in the book. I'm sure one small boy is very like another.'

'Thank goodness the ramblers found Harry. Do you know he told them some tale about Bryony being his dog?'

'Wishful thinking I suppose.'

'He's still desperate for a dog.' Jack ran a hand through his hair. 'I can't make him understand that he can't always have everything he wants and this time I mean what I say. The risks are too great.'

'He's very welcome to play with Bryony any time he likes. I mean,'

Sophie coloured up, 'if we're still speaking to each other that is.'

Jack gave a rueful smile. 'I'd almost forgotten about all that other business.'

'Have you heard from Emma?' Sophie asked.

Jack shook his head. 'She's gone to ground. She usually tells me where she is because she knows she can trust me, but this time she hasn't.'

'And it really is over between her and Iain?'

'Hm.' Jack looked pensive. 'I always thought he was a bit lightweight. I am sure there are things in his background he wouldn't want people to know about. Yet at the first sniff of trouble he dropped Emma like a hot potato.'

'Poor Emma. Did she really not want to speak to me either?'

'So she said, but perhaps she was too upset to think properly,' Jack tried to soften the blow. 'We all say things we don't mean when we've had a shock.'

'If it's any consolation, she's a survivor,' Sophie said.

'I hope so. I just wish I knew where she was, if only to reassure myself she's OK, but her unit's been in darkness for several days now. Even the press have given up prowling about the place.'

'That must be a great relief to Bill.'

'They were the bane of his life. Half the fencing round the back is going to have to be replaced from where it was damaged when someone tried to climb over it.'

'Do you think there's any truth in the rumours about Emma's father and Naomi Baxter?'

'I've no idea. I wouldn't have thought so. She was such a mousy little thing.'

'You knew her?' Sophie raised her eyebrows in shocked surprise.

'Only vaguely, our paths didn't really cross. She used to work in Roger Mountjoy's garage. She did the accounts. Didn't you know?'

Sophie shook her head. 'I had no idea.'

'I used to see her from time to time when I sloped off school to hang around the garage, but we never really spoke to each other. She always had her head down, adding up figures or something. I think she was shy.'

Jack put a hand across the starched tablecloth and touched Sophie's.

'Let's not talk about the Mountjoys.'

The subdued lighting of the dining area softened the harshness of Jack's jaw line. He was wearing a crisp white shirt, open at the neck.

'I seem to be forever in your debt, don't I?' His voice was soft and intimate.

'No.' Sophie tried to brush aside his words. She knew she also ought to remove her hand from Jack's touch but she lacked the willpower to move.

'I don't think I've had a moment's peace since I first met you,' Jack confessed. 'You were so infuriatingly candid and confrontational.'

'May I remind you the situation between us was not of my making?' Sophie was doing her best not to fall under the spell of his mesmerising brown eyes.

She'd noticed several admiring glances cast in his direction by other female diners. Until Sophie had seen him out of his boiler suit, she hadn't realised he possessed a certain rugged masculine charm which she was determined to withstand. She realised it wasn't going to be easy but their relationship was still too volatile for her to do otherwise.

'I only behaved as I did because of my feelings for Emma,' Jack confessed.

If Sophie needed a slap in the face to come to her senses, Jack's words had provided the necessary wake up call.

'I suppose I couldn't find it in myself to trust anyone new.'

Sophie's throat locked. There it was again. Emma was always the shadow between them.

'Then you should be pleased about what has happened to her.'

'Why?'

'Now she and Iain are no longer engaged, it leaves the field free for you.'

'I suppose it does.' Jack released Sophie's hand.

'After a suitable wait you can get engaged. People will soon forget all about Iain Buchanan.'

'Did Emma tell you that?'

'I haven't seen her since that night in the wine bar, and tell me what?' Sophie asked with a frown.

'That if she wasn't engaged to Iain she'd like to be engaged to me?'

'Not in so many words,' Sophie admitted. 'She actually told Iain there was nothing between you and her. She said you'd been on one or two dates but that's as far as things went.'

'And you didn't believe her?'

'It doesn't matter whether I did or not. You and she go back a long way, Jack. You've turned to each other in times of stress before. She may want to turn to you again now.'

'After my wife died,' Jack chose his words carefully, 'I did turn to Emma. I knew I could trust her to help me with Harry. I had my family of course, but Emma knew Linda so well. She was there the night we met. I know she's got this reputation of being a bit standoffish but she wasn't at all like that with Harry or me. Underneath it all she's got a heart of gold. She helped us through. I feel I ought to be helping her now. You do understand, don't you?'

'Yes,' Sophie nodded realising the bond between Jack and Emma was too strong for anyone to break.

The feelings that had prompted Jack to kiss Sophie down by the river when they had discovered Harry was safe were fuelled by nothing more than relief. At least on Jack's behalf it was relief. As for Sophie, the touch of his lips on hers had kindled feelings inside her she didn't know existed.

'Would you like some coffee?' Jack asked.

The dining area was emptying out and the waiters were beginning to clear the tables.

Sophie shook her head. 'I won't sleep,' she said, 'but thank you for the lovely meal. It was absolutely delicious.'

'We must do it again some time,' Jack

replied as he signalled for the bill.

'Yes, we must. My treat next time,' Sophie insisted. 'Perhaps Emma would like to come along too?'

'If she ever resurfaces.'

'I'm sure she will. She's got her clients to think of and I know she wouldn't want to let them down.'

Jack helped Sophie on with her jacket. As she straightened the cuffs, it felt as though Jack was stroking her shoulder. She half turned towards him, but the action brought her face too close to his and she immediately turned away again.

'If I can't tempt you to a cup of coffee would you like a nightcap at Riverside Cottage?' he murmured in her ear.

Sophie pretended to stifle a yawn. 'It's been a long day,' she said, covering her mouth with her hand. 'I really think I ought to have an early night. In fact if reception could call a taxi for me, I needn't trouble you to drive me home.'

She saw a muscle move as Jack

tightened his jaw. Sophie tossed back her head. Jack West could think what he liked, there was no way she was going to stand in as a substitute for Emma Mountjoy, and until the situation between Jack and Emma was official, that was all she would ever be — a substitute.

'If you're tired of my company I've no wish to keep you up.' His voice was clipped and tight.

They made their way towards the desk where Sophie ordered her taxi.

'You needn't wait,' Sophie insisted as Jack lingered by her side.

Now the evening was well and truly over, she wanted to go home and forget all about the man whose brown eyes branded her very soul.

'You'll let me know if Emma gets in touch with you?' she asked.

Jack nodded. 'And if you need any work done on your car, you know where to come.'

Her taxi drew up outside the front steps. Jack escorted her to the door.

His lips brushed against her cheek. 'Goodnight,' he said in a soft whisper.

Before Sophie could reply he disappeared in the direction of the car park. She climbed into the back seat of the taxi, her cheek still burning from the touch of his lips on her skin.

Sophie Discovers
More Letters

'Of course, dear, you'll be most welcome. Bring Bryony too.' Mary sounded pleased at Sophie's suggestion that they spend a lazy day together, sorting out her new shed. On the drive over to Berkham, Sophie made several stops at community centres and local libraries, to leave a pile of her leaflets.

In the past she had done talks and told people about her work. It always promoted a healthy interest in her agency and with time on her hands, Sophie decided it might be appropriate to approach the local authorities again.

Two weeks had passed since her dinner date with Jack and there had been no messages from either him or Emma, and Sophie had now to presume that part of her life was closed. The tabloids had moved on from Iain Buchanan. Another high profile story had taken its place and interest in Iain and Emma had faded. Sophie was sorry she had not been given the chance to apologise to Emma in person. She wasn't sure if she had been at fault but the fact remained it had been her notes that had sparked off the story, with disastrous results.

Sophie turned down by Berkham's war memorial and drove carefully along Church Street until she reached Mary's cottage. Before she had turned off her engine the front door was open. Bryony barked and poked her nose out of the window as Mary hurried down the drive to greet them.

'You're on time, how lovely. I was scared you'd get some important international telephone call and be whisked away at short notice on a mega important case.'

'Mary,' Sophie chided her, 'I think you're overrating my abilities.'

'Not at all.' Mary kissed her on the cheek as Bryony jumped out of the car and sniffed at the older woman's sandals. 'Belgian chocolates,' she accepted Sophie's gift with a smile, 'naughty but my absolute favourite. We'll have one later. Now come along in. I've made a batch of scones and coffee's all ready. We'll have it on the terrace. Listen to me,' she twittered. 'Don't I sound grand, elevenses on the terrace? I'll be wearing a huge hat soon and asking you if you've come far.' Mary laughed at herself. 'Come along in. You too, Bryony.'

A small shed had been erected in the sunniest part of the garden. It fronted onto a paved patio.

'I did the side trellises myself,' Mary explained. 'It can get a bit windy in that corner sometimes and the wind-breaks offer protection. I'm going to plant a fig tree up the side when I've sorted myself out. It's early days yet and I'm full of plans. Come and sit down. I don't know if we'll need the sunshade but I'll put it up to be on the safe side. You hear so much about protecting your skin from the sun these days, don't you?

And with your fair complexion, Sophie, we don't want you getting burnt.'

'I'll do it,' Sophie offered as Mary bustled off to get the coffee.

A day of Mary's friendly chatter was exactly what Sophie needed to clear her head. She didn't want to think about actors or garage mechanics, broken engagements or small boys with grubby faces. She missed Harry so much it hurt to think about him. Sophie knew she was being silly. She had only known the child for a short time, but he had wormed his way into her heart.

'Here we are.' Mary deposited a tray on the garden table. 'Help yourself.'

'This is really lovely,' Sophie said as she took a deep bite of a scone coated with thick homemade blackberry jam.

'Isn't it? I've taken to sitting out here of an evening and enjoying the coolest part of the day and reading my newspaper.'

A light breeze disturbed the over-hanging apple tree, scattering blossom over the lawn.

'I really should cut it back, but I

haven't had time. So,' Mary turned her attention back to Sophie. 'What are you doing now?' she asked.

'In theatrical terms, I'm resting,' Sophie replied.

'Am I allowed to ask about Emma or is it, what's that legal term, sub judice?'

'There's nothing really to tell you, Mary.'

'I only wondered how your friend was. I'm not interested in any of the nasty details that appeared in the press.'

'I haven't seen her,' Sophie replied.

'I don't know if you know, but Iain Buchanan's part has been temporarily written out of his soap opera. They've said he's away on holiday or something. It's one of those storylines that could develop or be left to fade out if his contract isn't renewed. There's even a new love interest for his deputy, so perhaps that part is being made up to take Iain's place.'

'I didn't know you were a fan,' Sophie said.

Mary flushed as she confessed, 'I

must admit I do watch it. I know it isn't very challenging viewing but I enjoy it. It helps me complete the crossword.'

Sophie laughed. 'It can't be a bad thing then, can it?'

'What about Mr West?' Mary asked with an innocent looked in her eyes. 'Jack wasn't it?'

'I haven't seen him either.'

'I thought the pair of you were good friends.'

'We were, but now Emma, Miss Mountjoy, is no longer engaged to Iain, well, they're an item.'

Mary raised her eyebrows. 'Really? You do surprise me. I wouldn't have thought Emma was Jack's type at all.'

'You don't know Emma, do you?' Sophie asked.

'No, but if a girl is engaged to Iain Buchanan, I would hardly have thought Jack West would have been her cup of tea. Sorry, dear, I don't mean to be rude, but the two men are very different. Iain's more, well, urbane.'

'Emma and Jack are old friends. Jack

used to work in her uncle's garage. That's how they met.'

'That reminds me,' Mary said, 'I've still got all that paperwork,' she lowered her voice, 'you know, from number three, down the road? Would you like it? I don't really want it. It's cluttering up my spare room and right now I need all the space I can get. I'll go and get it, shall I?' Mary leapt to her feet and scuttled off across the grass before Sophie could stop her.

Sophie leaned back and let the sunshine play on her face. She didn't want Mary's paperwork either but she acknowledged it wasn't fair to leave it with her. She supposed it did belong in Emma's file. Sophie usually kept them open for six months but this one she decided she would close as soon as she got back to her flat. There would be no further developments and she couldn't keep it open forever.

'Here we are.' Mary's cheerful voice disturbed Sophie's snooze in the sunshine.

'There's a lot of it.' Sophie looked in dismay at the boxes Mary had deposited at her feet.

'I gather it was hidden in a corner of the loft behind an old chest or something. No-one thought to look there before. I've read some of it, but to be honest it's all a bit dull. By the end of the evening I was yawning my head off. You may find something of interest. If you don't can you keep it in your archives?'

'I'll take it off your hands.' Sophie felt duty bound to offer.

'Why don't you sit there and enjoy another cup of coffee while I fix lunch?'

'I thought we were going out.'

'I've got us a little treat. The fish van was parked on the green yesterday and he had some delicious fresh crab. I bought two. I thought we could have them with hot new potatoes and a salad?'

'That's lovely, Mary, but you must let me contribute.'

'Nonsense. I love having company

and there's really nothing to do, apart from cook the potatoes. I can chat to you through my kitchen window while I'm doing them. You need looking after Sophie and I shall of course expect you to eat every scrap of food on your plate. We've got strawberry shortcake for dessert, another of my specialities.'

'You shouldn't have gone to so much trouble,' Sophie protested.

'No trouble at all. When my husband was alive we were always entertaining. I quite miss it. Would you prefer to read my magazine rather than go through those dusty old papers?'

'I'd better battle through some of these,' Sophie said reluctantly. 'If I don't do it now, I may never get round to it.'

'I know the feeling, dear. Well, I'll leave you in peace. Can I tempt you to the last scone?'

'Not if I'm to leave some room for lunch,' Sophie replied.

She dragged one of the cardboard boxes towards her and lifted the lid. In the kitchen Mary clattered about with her saucepans while she listened to the radio.

The dust on the papers made Sophie sneeze. Most of the records appeared to be personal paperwork. Tony was a meticulous record keeper and everything was there. All his household bills were annotated with the date he had paid them and the number of the cheque. The cottage was leased from a local agency and it seemed Tony had lived there for about four years. There wasn't much reference to Naomi and none at all to Adam.

Despite the dullness of the records, Sophie was intrigued. Where had Naomi been living before she moved in with her brother? And why had she moved in with him? There was no diary so Sophie wasn't sure of the exact dates but from what she knew about Tony's disappearance, she would guess they had been together for no longer than a few months.

On top of the pile of papers had been

a copy of Tony's letter of resignation to the Council. Judging from the formality of the letter, Sophie wondered if he had been asked to resign, rather than face the disgrace of being dismissed. She also wondered if the rumours about bribery were true. It hardly seemed to fit in with the meticulous character of the man.

She rifled through a few more sheets of paper. There was absolutely nothing to connect the Baxters with Sir Gerald Mountjoy. If Emma hadn't found the cuttings and the lock of baby hair, no-one would have suspected any connection between the two families.

'It's ready,' Mary called through the open kitchen window.

'I'll come and get it. Stay there.' Sophie was glad to have a reason to stand up. She was beginning to get cramp in her legs.

She crammed the rest of the paperwork back in the box and nudged it under the garden table with her foot.

'Fresh crab has always been a

weakness of mine,' Mary confided as they set out the table.'

'This mayonnaise is delicious,' Sophie complimented Mary.

'Made to another of my own recipes,' Mary boasted. 'So did you find anything of interest?' She nodded towards the discarded boxes.

'Nothing at all. I can understand why the police were perplexed. To all intents and purposes the Baxters were a thoroughly normal family.'

'I agree. It just shows that you never really know what goes on behind locked doors, do you?'

Mary began to clear away the plates. 'I can manage,' she insisted, brushing away Sophie's efforts to help.

'I really don't think I can manage any more,' Sophie insisted as she spooned up the last mouthful of Mary's strawberry shortcake.

'Surely you've got room for some coffee and one of your Belgian chocolates after I've done the washing up?'

'Only if you let me help,' Sophie

insisted, firmly taking the tray out of Mary's hands. 'You've done enough.'

'If you insist,' Mary replied. 'Doing the dishes does seem to go quicker when there are two of you I must admit.'

'I'll load those boxes into my car,' Sophie said as Mary wiped down the draining board after they'd put the last plate in the cupboard.

'Right, I'll get the kettle on. You can go out the side gate, dear. I've unlatched it and it's an easier way round and a lot quicker.'

Bryony began barking wildly as Sophie loaded the last of the boxes into the boot of her car.

'Quiet,' she reprimanded her. 'We don't want to upset Mary's neighbours.'

'What is it?' Sophie complained as Bryony began tugging at her skirt.

She slammed down the boot and locked it. The two of them almost fell over each other as Bryony raced in front of Sophie and ran down the side entrance to Mary's cottage.

'Mary,' Sophie shrieked as she saw her friend spread eagled on the lawn, the coffee cups smashed to smithereens on the terrace. 'Can you hear me?'

Mary groaned. 'My ankle. I tripped.'

'Stay there. I'm calling for an ambulance.'

'Doctor,' Mary mumbled. 'No need for hospital. Such a fuss.'

'What's his number?'

'Don't know.'

'Bryony, keep guard,' Sophie ordered.

Unable to get a signal on her mobile, Sophie ran to the far corner of the garden. Breathless with shock she stumbled over her request for an ambulance.

'There's been an incident on the motorway,' the operator replied. 'The emergency services are fully stretched at the moment and there are long delays all round. If the patient is mobile can you drive her to the hospital yourself?'

Heart in her mouth, Sophie rang off then raced back to where Mary was still lying on the lawn, to tell her the news.

A Friendship Rekindled

The forecourt of the accident and emergency department outside the hospital was swarming with vehicles and patients.

'I'm all right, dear,' Mary insisted. 'There was no need for all this bother. I'm sure a bag of frozen peas on my ankle would have done the trick.'

Now she had recovered from the shock, Mary was busy apologising for all the fuss her fall had caused.

'You need to get your ankle x-rayed,' Sophie insisted.

'It does seem to have swollen rather a lot,' Mary looked down at her injury. 'So silly of me. I wasn't looking where I was going and the next moment my leg had gone from under me. I'm sorry to put you to so much trouble.'

'Don't be silly, Mary, and it's no trouble. Are you sure you're comfortable?'

The only suitable footwear they could find was an old slipper. After Sophie had cut the back out Mary had been able to put it on and with Sophie's help hobble to the car. Mary was now stretched out on the back seat with a stack of comfortable cushions supporting her back. Sophie was worried Bryony might jog Mary's ankle, so they had been forced to lock her up in the kitchen.

'Look at all these people,' Mary said as Sophie inched her car nearer the reception area. There were still several vehicles in the queue in front of them. 'I've never seen anything like it.'

She didn't want to worry Mary, but Sophie knew, despite her friend's robust protestations to the contrary, they were going to have difficulty manoeuvring her into the building. There was no way Mary could manage on her own, but parking space was at a premium and Sophie didn't know what she was going to do once they reached arrivals. Sophie was forced to resist the temptation to abandon her car in one of the emergency bays that were empty now, but reserved for medical staff and ambulances.

'Good heavens.' Mary leaned forward and grabbed Sophie's arm making her jump. 'Are my eyes deceiving me or is that your gentleman friend?'

'What? Where?'

'Look, over there. He's coming towards us.'

Sophie could hardly believe her eyes. Battling his way through the throngs of patients was the unmistakeable figure of Jack West. Despite the frown scarring his forehead, Sophie was filled with relief at the sight of him. She wound down her window.

'What are you doing here?' he demanded.

'I could ask you the same question,' Sophie replied.

'Were you caught up in the motorway incident?' Jack's eyes searched Sophie's face. 'Have you been injured?' he asked in a sharp voice.

'No, of course not. My friend Mary, you remember Mary?' Sophie indicated her passenger in the back seat.

'Hello, dear,' Mary waved majestically from her reclined position. 'We met at the garden centre when I was looking at sheds? I'm afraid I'm the cause of all the trouble. I tripped over some steps and I've twisted my ankle, such a silly thing to happen. Then we couldn't get an ambulance because something had happened on the motor-way so Sophie's driven me all the way over here, and now we don't know where we're going to park. Is it always this busy?'

'Don't move. I'll get you a wheel-chair.' Jack took charge of the situation. 'Then I'll park your car, Sophie while you escort Mary inside.'

He headed towards the automatic doors that led to the reception area before Sophie could protest.

'At the risk of sounding old-fashioned, dear, it's so nice to have a man take charge of the situation, isn't it? They're always better at organising things like this, aren't they?'

'We could have managed,' Sophie insisted with a mutinous jut of her jaw, 'there was no need for Jack to interfere.'

Mary raised her eyebrows at the sharp tone of Sophie's voice.

'If you say so,' she agreed mildly, 'although I have to admit I wasn't looking forward to struggling down hospital corridors on my own while you parked the car.'

Sophie realised she was behaving childishly and flushed in embarrassment.

'You're quite right, Mary, I'm sorry. I didn't mean to sound ungrateful. Seeing Jack again was a bit of a shock that's all.'

'And here he is, back already with a wheelchair.'

The relief in Mary's voice was obvious and Sophie felt further ashamed of herself.

'Lean on me, Mary,' Jack instructed her.

'Are you sure you don't mind parking

the car?' Sophie asked, reluctant to part with her keys. Surrendering them to Jack was in some ways akin to surrendering her independence.

'I won't be long,' he insisted, adjusting the front driver's seat to accommodate his long legs. 'You go on ahead and I'll come and find you inside. The nurse on the desk is expecting you.'

Sophie was sitting alone on one of the blue plastic chairs, nursing a cup of machine-dispensed coffee by the time Jack finally returned. She saw female heads turn in his direction as the automatic doors slid open. Despite his slight limp Jack was still the most charismatic man present and Sophie felt an unaccustomed thrill of pleasure at seeing him again. She sat up straight and tried not to look too eager. She must remember his relationship with Emma and that she had no rights on him.

'How is Mary?' Jack asked as he sat down beside her.

'She's having an x-ray done now. Thank you for everything.'

His crooked smile softened the anxiety in his face. 'Sorry I was so long. It took me a while to find a parking space. Your car is over by the admin block. Here are your keys.'

'Thank you. Er, at the risk of sounding ungrateful, you don't have to stay.'

' 'Fraid I do,' Jack admitted with a rueful smile. 'If you don't want me to sit here I can go over there.' He nodded towards a vacant seat on other side of the waiting area.

Sophie experienced a nasty thumping sensation in her chest.

'What do you mean you have to stay?'

'That accident on the motorway,' Jack began.

'Were you involved?' Jack winced as she dug her fingernails into his arm. 'Is that why you're here?'

'No, it isn't.'

'It's not Harry is it?'

'Harry's fine,' Jack assured her. 'He's with his grandmother and the last I heard they were re-decorating the kitchen a fetching shade of chocolate cake mix. So if you'll unhand me and let me get on with my explanation?'

'Sorry,' Sophie apologised.

'Thank you.' Jack squeezed her fingers, as he looked deep into her eyes. Sophie withdrew her hand from his and sipped at her gritty coffee hoping he wouldn't notice her rising colour.

'You were saying?' she prompted.

'What was I saying?' Jack frowned in a distracted manner.

'The accident?'

'Right. Yes. The police telephoned and asked if I could help clear the road. Some cars had swerved to avoid a lorry that had shed its load over the carriage-way and wound up stranded by the barrier, sort of facing the wrong direction. One or two people suffered minor injuries, cuts and bruises, that sort of thing, but to be on the safe side the emergency services insisted everyone was checked over.'

'That still doesn't explain why you're

here,' Sophie's voice was still faint with concern.

Jack made a face. 'It's a bit embarrassing really. One of the cars I was asked to move had an automatic gearbox and my feet got in a bit of a tangle with the pedals.' He made a face. 'It's not something I would tell everyone but I squashed my bad toes. I tried telling the paramedics I was fine, but I got scooped up with everyone else. As I was getting out of the ambulance I saw you and Mary in the queue behind us.'

'So you're waiting for an x-ray too?'

'I was, but I think I've lost my place in the queue.'

'To Mary?'

'Probably,' Jack admitted cheerfully, 'I had a word with the girl on the desk when I came to get a wheelchair and they agreed Mary could take advantage of the gap in the schedule.'

'You didn't have to do that,' Sophie insisted.

'No sense in both of us missing out,'

Jack replied with a cheerful smile. 'I'm not really sure I should be here anyway. I feel a bit of a fraud. My foot doesn't hurt at all but Mary's ankle doesn't look too clever.'

'We were having lunch,' Sophie admitted, 'and while I was loading up the car with,' she hesitated, 'some papers, Mary made the coffee. Bryony began barking like mad and when we went back into the garden we found her.'

'Poor old Mary,' Jack sympathised. 'So, how are you?' he asked.

'Fine,' Sophie answered automatically, remembering the circumstances of their last meeting.

'Keeping busy?'

'Always lots to do.' It was getting more and more difficult to keep smiling at Jack and Sophie wished he wouldn't look at her quite so intently as if he was trying to memorise every detail of her face.

The breeze in Mary's garden had mussed up her hair and she was pretty sure in all the excitement her eye make up had run.

'How's Emma?' she asked, hoping the mention of her name would erect a barrier between herself and Jack.

'She's back from her holiday,' he said slowly.

'Have you seen her?'

'Once or twice. She's been working hard, anxious to make up her backlog.'

'Do you have any idea how things are between her and Iain?' Sophie asked careful not to betray too much of her feelings.

'He hasn't bothered us at The Stable Yard recently, much to Bill's relief.'

'I really am very sorry for what happened,' Sophie repeated, 'do you think Emma would speak to me now if I gave her a call and tried to explain? I mean things have calmed down a bit haven't they?'

'I should leave it,' Jack replied. 'Least said soonest mended, don't you think?'

'Mr West?' The nurse called over.

He looked up.

'You're next,' she said.

'Will you be here when I get through?' Jack asked as he got to his feet.

'That depends on Mary,' Sophie replied.

'Then can I call you?' he asked. 'I know our dinner dates tend to be fraught experiences, but I'd like to give it another go, if you're willing?'

'What about Emma?'

'She won't mind.'

'If you're sure?' Sophie still hesitated. 'Perhaps she would like to come along as well? I did promise it would be my treat the next time we had dinner together.'

'I don't want to have dinner with Emma,' Jack said, ignoring the looks from the impatient nurse who was waiting to take him through to x-ray, 'I want to have dinner with you. Are you always this hard to date?' he demanded.

Aware of the several interested expressions now being cast in their direction, Sophie mumbled, 'You've got my number.' Then feeling she was being less than gracious, she managed to smile, 'I think dinner would be a great idea.'

Jack's answering smile left her with a warm feeling inching up her spine.

'Then I'll give you a call.'

'Just a bad wrench, dear,' Mary said as she appeared a few moments later with a stoutly bandaged ankle. 'I've got to keep as much weight off it as possible for the next week or so, but no permanent damage done.'

'Right, well,' Sophie beamed at her. 'Back home then?'

'You're looking a lot happier, I must say,' Mary responded.

'It's the relief knowing you haven't fractured your ankle. You wait here while I go and fetch the car.'

Mary looked round. 'Where's Jack?'

'He's gone through to have his foot x-rayed. He squashed his toes under a pedal on one of the cars he was moving.'

'I wanted to thank him. Do you know

he gave up his place in the queue for me?'

'He did mention it, yes.'

Mary hesitated. 'Did you mean what you said about you and him not being an item?'

'Mary, I appreciate what you're trying to do, but believe me, there is nothing between myself and Jack West.'

For the moment there was no need to tell her about Jack's dinner invitation. In fact Sophie would rather she didn't know at all.

Mary broke into a relieved smile.

'In that case it's good news about Jack and Emma Mountjoy isn't it? I wasn't sure how you'd take it, but if there's nothing between you, well, you won't mind will you?'

'What news?' Sophie asked. 'What won't I mind?'

'They were talking about it in the x-ray department. Apparently one of the nurses on duty knows Emma. I don't know if it's official, but she seemed to think it was.'

'Mary, what are you talking about?'

'Didn't I say? Jack and Emma Mount-joy? Now things have fallen through with Iain Buchanan they're secretly engaged. Isn't that wonderful news?'

Sophie Meets A Mystery Man

Now Emma was no longer in the public eye, her engagement was only a small announcement on an inner page of the papers. The local Gazette published a photo of Jack and Emma smiling into each other's eyes as they stood on the steps outside the golf club. A diamond sparkled on the third finger of Emma's left hand.

Sophie forced herself to read the article.

The happy couple had celebrated the news with a quiet dinner in the renowned Vista Lounge restaurant that overlooks the floodlit range, the report read. Emma was sporting an antique engagement ring and seemed to have recovered from her unfortunate affair with the famous actor, Iain Buchanan.

239

The couple enjoyed the Vista Lounge's signature menu of a fresh baby vegetables starter, followed by lobster salad. A bottle of champagne was presented to them, courtesy of the Gazette.

'Jack and I are old friends,' Miss Mountjoy informed our reporter.

Mr Buchanan's agent says whilst there is no comment from her client, who is in America on business, she is sure he wishes them both well and every happiness in their future life together.

Sophie let the answer phone take all her messages. To think she had been foolish enough to believe Jack was serious when he had suggested dinner together, when all the time he had been secretly engaged to Emma.

'Come on, Bryony,' Sophie picked up her lead. 'We need to jog.'

The air on the common was refreshing and Sophie completed two circuits of the lake before taking a breather. She leant forward, her hands on her thighs trying not to remember that this was where it had all begun, except today there was no sound of thundering hooves in the background. Emma would be too busy planning her forthcoming wedding.

Sophie looked round. Judging from the number of model boats on the lake, it looked as though she had stumbled across the annual general meeting of the local miniature sailing club. She was surrounded by excited males of all ages discussing the merits of sail against motor power.

'Excuse me.'

A voice behind her made her jump.

'Yes?'

A bespectacled young man wearing a suit and tie and looking rather over-dressed in the relaxed surroundings of the park, smiled at her.

'Do you live in Steepways?'

'Can I help you?' she asked by way of reply.

'I'm looking for The Manor House. Do you know where it is?'

Sophie blinked. 'Are you a reporter?' she asked.

'I'm sorry?' The man looked confused by her question.

'Only if you are, you've missed the boat. Emma Mountjoy doesn't live there any more. She hasn't lived there for over a year now.'

'Did you say Emma Mountjoy?'

'Yes, as in was engaged to Iain Buchanan.'

'You mean the television actor?' The glasses were now working overtime as the man tried to take in all that Sophie was saying.

'So if you're looking for a story, you're too late. Emma's now engaged to Jack West and Iain Buchanan's gone after a film part in America. Was there anything else you needed to know?'

'I see, er, well, thank you,' the young man said with a puzzled smile.

Sophie frowned. The man did look lost. She bit her lip. Perhaps he was looking for one of the new tenants of The Manor House. After Emma's aunt had sold up, a property developer had converted the house into several luxury apartments, aimed specifically at the young professional commuter.

'The Manor's on the other side of town,' she relented. 'Sorry, I didn't mean to snap. You're not a reporter are you?'

'No, I'm not. Well thank you for your help.' He now looked anxious to get away.

Sophie watched him hurry off. Bryony hadn't barked at the stranger, which was odd. Her tail had thumped companionably against the calf of Sophie's leg throughout their encounter, which would mean she hadn't seen the man as a threat.

There was something about the man that seemed familiar to Sophie, but she couldn't quite grasp what it was. He was blond and the white of his shirt had reflected his slightly sun tanned fair skin. The suit had been tailored in the Continental manner and Sophie wondered if he lived abroad. His English was fluent, which suggested he had spent some time in this country, thought Sophie.

Back at the flat, she checked her calls.

'Hello, dear.' It was Mary's voice. 'Just to let you know my ankle's recovering nicely. I'm staying with my daughter and grandson for a few days. It's lovely to be waited on. Today I had breakfast in bed. We never did get round to having our cup of coffee with one of your nice chocolates, did we? Shall we make it a date for when I get back?

'By the way,' she went on, 'did you read in the Gazette, about Jack and Emma's engagement? They make a lovely couple, don't they? I'll be in touch when I get home. Goodbye, dear.'

Sophie switched to the next message.

'Sophie, we have to talk.'

She didn't bother listening to the rest of Jack's message. Whatever he had to say, she wasn't interested.

'Ms Blaze?' Sophie listened to the

third message. 'My name is Garcia. I would like to make an appointment to meet you. Perhaps I could call round later this evening? I know it's short notice, but I'm only in the country for a few days and I need to talk to you. I obtained your telephone number from one of your flyers when I visited the library for a map of the area. If you could give me your address, I would be most grateful.'

Sophie left a message on Mr Garcia's voice mail informing him she was in all evening and that she would be pleased to see him any time. Hopefully, she thought, it would be a new case.

Sophie decided to tidy up the office area before her visitor arrived. She usually conducted her business meetings in a corner of the living room but Mary's boxes littered all available floor space. Sophie still hadn't got round to sorting them out. She glanced at her watch. There wasn't time now. Opening a cupboard door, she thrust them inside. The lid fell off one of them and several sheets of paper fluttered to the floor. She glanced at them. They appeared to be more bills, and a photocopy of a passport application form. Sophie glanced at it. If the family had moved abroad it would perhaps explain why the police had not been able to trace them.

Locking the door and dismissing all thoughts of the Baxters from her mind, Sophie set about tidying her desk. Having a purpose again stopped her thinking about Jack West.

Surprised to see it was eight o'clock in the evening before she finally finished, Sophie decided there was just time to have a quick shower before her client arrived. Standing under the hot spray, she tried to decide what to wear. Mr Garcia had sounded young, so perhaps an informal approach would be appropriate.

Drying her hair she decided to go for a cream T shirt and summer skirt. After making a few adjustments in the mirror, Sophie was satisfied with her appearance. She wasn't vain, but she knew how important image was, especially for a first meeting.

A warm breeze through the open balcony window lured her onto her little terrace. The evening was warm and it was a perfect time to water her pot plants. Engrossed in her task, she almost didn't hear the front door bell ring.

'Out of the way, Bryony,' she shooed her dog back into her basket. 'Remember, no barking. This is business.'

She opened the door. Her smile of welcome froze on her lips. Standing outside her flat was the fair-haired man she had met on the common.

'You?' She said. 'How did you find out where I lived?'

'You left a message in my voice mail,' he replied with a pleasant smile. 'There's no need to look so worried. My name is Garcia. I'm your evening appointment.' He put out his hand to shake hers. 'How do you do. May I come in?'

The Truth At Last

'I'm sorry, Mr Garcia,' Sophie began, nervously fingering the door chain and wishing she'd thought to leave it secured. It was one of the basic rules of private detecting — never leave yourself vulnerable. 'I don't think we can do business.'

'Would it take the worried look off your face if I told you my first name is Adam and that my business with you is legitimate?'

'I don't see what your first name has to do with anything.' Sophie said then frowned. 'Did you say Adam?'

'As in Baxter?'

'You're Adam Baxter, Naomi's son?'

'I am,' he smiled shyly, adding, 'I wasn't tailing you on the common and I can assure you I'm not a stalker. I had no idea who I was talking to when I bumped into you. I was looking for The Manor House because that's where my mother said the Mountjoy family lived.'

'I see.' Sophie opened the door wider, feeling more than a little foolish. 'I'm sorry I didn't mean to be discourteous. You took me by surprise, that's all.'

'I was surprised to see you too. I wasn't going to bother you, but when I got to The Manor House I realised it had been converted into flats. You were my only other lead.'

'You'd better come in.'

'What a lovely flat,' he looked round in appreciation as the sunlight cast a dying beam across Sophie's newly polished desk. He sniffed appreciatively. 'Do I smell lavender?'

'It was a trick I picked up from an old school friend,' she admitted, thinking briefly of Emma. 'It makes a welcoming smell, especially at this time of day when everyone is feeling a bit tired.'

'Nothing beats an English evening does it?' Adam smiled at her, a smile that again puzzled Sophie. There was something very familiar about it.

'Have we met before?' she asked Adam.

'I don't think so. Why?'

She shook her head. 'Sorry, it's been a trying time lately. I think I'm beginning to imagine things. Would you like a drink?'

'Thank you.'

'Make yourself comfortable.'

When Sophie returned Adam Baxter was seated on one of the easy chairs on the balcony and enjoying the last of the day.

'I hope you don't mind me sitting out here?'

'Not at all. I often enjoy the sunset.'

'Where I come from it's too hot to sit outside. The sun is too strong for my skin. I'm always getting burnt or bitten by bugs. Here it's different.'

'Where do you live?' Sophie poured out two glasses of lemonade.

'Southern Spain.'

'That explains the tan.' She passed a glass over to Adam.

'I don't think my English complexion will ever get used to the Spanish sunshine.'

'So what brings you to Steepways?' Sophie enquired.

'I hardly know where to start.' Adam put his glass back down on the table. 'It's all a bit complicated really and I'm only coming to terms with some of it myself,' he said with his shy smile.

'You mentioned the Mountjoy family. Was that why were you looking for The Manor House?' Sophie tried nudging the interview into a positive direction.

'I was hoping to find Emma Mountjoy and that address was the only contact I had. By the way what was all that you were saying about reporters and Iain Buchanan?'

'Emma was briefly engaged to Iain Buchanan,' Sophie dismissed his question with a gesture of her hands. 'The press have been making a bit of a nuisance of themselves. I'm sorry I thought you were one of them. I should have known from the suit and your neat appearance that you weren't a reporter.'

Adam grimaced at he looked down at his attire. 'Do you mind if I take off my jacket? I'm not used to wearing formal clothes, but I'm over here on business and I've been at a meeting in London all day. There wasn't time to change and as I'm due to fly home to Spain tomorrow, this was the only window I had to come down here.'

'I see,' Sophie replied, not really understanding what was going on.

'My mother told me you were interested in knowing what had happened to us. She gets the Gazette sent out to a poste restante and I understand there was an article about Emma?' He frowned. 'Did I get it wrong? I thought my mother said Emma's fiancé was called Jack not Iain?'

'It's a long story,' Sophie sighed. 'How did you find out about me?'

A shadow crossed Adam's face. 'I don't know anything about you. That's why it's so difficult to know where to start.' He paused. 'I've tried thinking things through since my mother's telephone call, but everything's still a bit of a jumble. She wasn't making much sense and I only had my scribbled notes to go on. You know those pads they give you by the bed in hotel rooms? I ran out of paper halfway through our conversation.' Adam took a deep breath, 'and I've had to try to remember the rest.'

'Take your time,' Sophie urged him.

'My mother subscribes to a clipping service. They send her everything to do with Steepways. Although we've lived in Spain for years, she still gets homesick. That's why she takes the Gazette.'

'I understand.'

'Post can be a bit irregular in the village where we live so we use the poste restante address. That means we have to go and get our mail from our box when we go into town. Are you with me so far?'

Sophie nodded.

'We've had hotter weather than usual

this year and although it's only the beginning of the season, people have been staying indoors as much as possible. We live in a small village north of Estepona, that's in Andalusia. Have you been to Spain?' Adam asked.

'We flew to Gibraltar once, before we went on to Tangiers on a school trip, many years ago.'

'We are not too far from the rock, so you know roughly where I live. Sorry, I seem to have got a bit sidetracked don't I? Where was I?'

'Your mother's clipping service?'

'Yes. Right. My mother hasn't been very well recently and she hasn't been going into town to collect her post as frequently as usual. When she did she found a huge envelope of clippings. She sometimes goes for months without anything so you can imagine it was a bit of a surprise to her. She rang me at my hotel last night to tell me a private detective was looking for us. She was very worried.'

'There's nothing to worry about,' Sophie assured him.

'She's always been a bit nervy and I think she panicked.'

'Please assure your mother she isn't in any trouble.'

'She will be relieved.'

'I had a private arrangement with Emma Mountjoy to see what I could find out about you, but unfortunately some of my notes got into the wrong hands and an unscrupulous reporter used them as the basis for an article. Emma had great news value at the time and the whole thing was blown out of all proportion.'

'Do you mind if I give my mother a quick call on my mobile? To reassure her?'

'Of course not. I'll make us some sandwiches, shall I?' Sophie stood up, anxious not to eavesdrop on such a personal conversation. 'Do you like cheese and tomato?' she asked.

'Love them,' he smiled back at her in his faintly disturbing way, leaving Sophie more than ever convinced they had met somewhere before.

The light was going from the day by the time Adam had finished his call and Sophie had made the sandwiches. They moved indoors to eat their scratch supper at Sophie's oak table.

'I was only a baby when we moved to Spain,' Adam explained. 'I've always spoken English to my mother, but at times I feel more Spanish than English. My second family was Spanish and I grew up in Spain so the Spanish language comes as naturally to me as does English.'

'Why do you call yourself Adam Garcia?' Sophie asked.

'My mother married a man called Carlos Garcia when I was about six and I adopted his name. It was just after my uncle died so it made sense. It was easier from a legal point of view as well.'

'I am right in thinking your uncle was Tony Baxter?'

'Yes,' he nodded.

'Do you know why your family moved to Spain at such short notice?'

'I think it was something to do with

my uncle's health. My mother never really said but Uncle Tony did have a poor chest and the English winters took their strain on him. So he decided to take up a job in Spain. There was plenty of work teaching English in the local schools.'

'Do you know of any family connection to the Mountjoys?' Sophie asked carefully.

Adam sipped his coffee. 'Yes, I do,' he admitted.

'You do?' Sophie sat up straight.

'When I told you my name was Adam Baxter, that wasn't strictly true.'

Sophie fiddled with the envelope of cuttings Emma had left with her. She picked up the lock of baby hair. Now she knew to whom it belonged and why she thought she recognised Adam Baxter. He and Emma shared the same smile.

'My real name is Adam Mountjoy.'

Down in the street someone slammed a car door. Sophie heard the car start up and drive away. Disturbed by the noise Bryony padded across the floor and snuffled up to Sophie's feet.

'Say something,' Adam urged as the silence between them lengthened.

'Your father was Gerald Mountjoy?'

Adam shook his head. 'No. My father's name was Roger Mountjoy.'

'What?' Sophie asked in shock.

'My mother met him when she used to do the books for him at his garage.'

Sophie remembered Jack telling her he had seen Naomi working in the office.

'What's that you're holding?' Adam changed the subject as he leaned over and took the envelope containing the lock of baby hair out of Sophie's unresisting fingers.

'Emma found it amongst her father's things. I suppose your father gave it to him for safe keeping.'

'I was sorry my father and my uncle both died within such a short time of each other. I would have liked to have met them.' Adam inspected the contents of the envelope. 'Is this my hair?'

'I think it must be. Emma said it wasn't hers. That's why she called me in.'

'To find me?'

Sophie took a deep breath. 'I don't know how much you know about your family's move to Spain, but I believe it was rather sudden.' Sophie slid the newspaper cuttings out of sight under a file while Adam continued to study the lock of baby hair.

'Sorry,' he returned his attention to Sophie. 'May I keep this?'

'I'd have to ask Emma.'

'I understand.' Adam handed the envelope back to Sophie. 'Sorry, did you ask me something?'

'Do you know why your mother and uncle left for Spain so suddenly?'

'I always assumed it was for reason of my uncle's health, but I suppose it could have been because my mother wanted to get away as well.'

'To start a new life away from the Mountjoys?'

'My mother doesn't talk much about

her life in England and when she married Carlos she adopted Spanish nationality. The English side of my life sort of faded into the past. I often wondered about my real father. My mother would never talk much about him either.'

'Do you know if Roger Mountjoy acknowledged you as his son?'

'He is named as my father on my birth certificate. From what my mother has told me they married without his family's knowledge.'

'They were married?' Sophie echoed in surprise.

'I think, well,' Adam hesitated, 'she was in the first stages of pregnancy, but my mother was very young and rather inexperienced in the ways of the world and I don't think she was ready for marriage or a baby. From what she has said about them I don't think the Mountjoys really approved of her. She didn't come from their sort of world. She's always been a quiet sort of person. As I understand it, when the marriage crumbled under family pressure she came back to live with her brother. Then we moved out to Spain and built a life for ourselves out there.'

'It's a sad story.'

'It will have a happy outcome if I get to meet my cousin,' Adam smiled. 'What's Emma like?' he asked.

'You resemble her,' Sophie replied.

'Do you think she'll be pleased to learn she has a cousin?'

'I think she'll be absolutely delighted.'

Sophie was certain on that one. Emma had once told Sophie she envied her for having two brothers and a close knit happy family.

Adam glanced at his watch. 'It's getting late and I do have to drive back to London tonight. If I give you my email address, would you pass it on to Emma? I'd love to meet her the next time I'm over.'

He scribbled down a number on a scrap of paper. 'There's my mobile number too.' He stood up. 'Thank you for a lovely evening. You've put my mind at rest and my mother's too.' He paused by the door. 'I've often thought Mother's nerves were due to something that happened in England. She was always jumpy whenever we bumped into English visitors in Estepona and she often went out of her way to avoid them. She used to pretend she was Spanish. I used to put it down to her shyness. I know different now. She was trying to escape her past, I suppose.'

Sophie watched him disappear down the stairs and out into the night air. She still couldn't take in all that Adam had told her.

It was Roger Mountjoy, not Gerald, who had been married to Naomi Baxter. Adam was their son. She supposed he never really forgot his first wife and that was why he kept a lock of Adam's hair hidden away amongst the family's private papers. Gerald had kept in touch with Naomi and tried to help her find somewhere to live until circumstances forced her and her brother to move to Spain when all connection between the two families was severed.

Sophie felt a twinge of sadness now the mystery was solved. Perhaps Roger had intended keeping in touch with Naomi too, but their sudden disappearance meant he was unable to do so.

She looked at the rather sad little cuttings. All Tony Baxter was guilty of was going away without telling anyone of his plans, nothing else.

If Emma wanted to show her cousin the press cutting of what happened, then Sophie decided it was up to her. Sophie's involvement in the case was now officially finished.

She glanced at Adam's handwritten note. It was too late to call Emma's number now with the news. She would have to tell her of course, and what she had to say was far too personal to put into an email. That meant only one thing. She would have to visit Stable Yard. Her stomach tightened. There was no way she could avoid seeing Jack West again, but if she did, she wasn't sure she would remain in control of her emotions.

Thrusting the press cuttings back into their envelope, together with the baby hair and Adam's telephone number, Sophie decided she would think about what to do in the morning.

She fell asleep the moment her head touched the pillow.

'Your Daddy's Engaged To Emma'

The doors to unit 6B were wide open. Sophie's heart sank at the sight of another classic car on the forecourt. The bonnet was up indicating that someone had been working on it. Sophie looked round. The forecourt was deserted and there was no sign of Jack but that morning there had been two more urgent messages from him on her answer phone.

Sophie had slept so soundly after Adam's visit she hadn't heard the telephone ring. She had erased both of the messages without listening to them. Nothing Jack West had to say would interest her.

She could hear a radio playing in the background. It was tuned to Jack's favourite classical music channel. That meant he had to be around somewhere. Sophie decided it wouldn't be wise to linger.

She glanced over her shoulder. Emma's studio was in darkness. Sophie bit her lip in exasperation. Nothing was going to plan. If Emma were out then all her careful planning would be for nothing. She had timed her visit to coincide with Harry's school run but all she had succeeded in doing was engineering a potential showdown with Jack.

She clutched her envelope. Inside were Emma's father's newspapers cuttings, the lock of baby hair and a full report of Sophie's meeting with Adam, and all his contact details. She could she supposed post it through Emma's letterbox, but she wanted to be sure Emma read the contents. She knew from experience her friend was lax when it came to paperwork. She would probably toss the envelope to one side intending to read the contents at a later date and then forget all about them.

'Sophie.'

While Sophie was still debating what to do she heard a delighted cry in the background and the next moment an excited pair of sturdy arms clutched out at her legs, nearly dragging her down to the ground.

'Where've you been?'

She recovered her balance and looked down into Harry's smiling face. His expression clutched at her heart. She didn't think it was possible to love someone else's child as much as she loved Harry, but the little rascal was as dear to her as her own nephews. She smiled back at him. If only his father's love for her could be as unconditional.

'Hello, darling.' She stroked his oil-stained cheek. 'Don't tell me you've bunked off school again? This is getting to be a bad habit.' She tried to look stern, but her expression didn't really work.

'Half term this week. I'm helping Daddy in the garage. Where've you been?' he repeated.

'I've been very busy.'

'Daddy's been ringing you lots of times and he's very cross because you didn't ring back. He was going to visit you but Granny's in Canada visiting my aunties and Emma's not here so he had no-one to leave me with. I wanted to come too but he said it was grown up stuff he wanted to talk to you about.' Harry made a face.

'Where is Emma?' Sophie asked, in the vain hope that Harry might know where she was.

'On holiday.'

'I thought she was back.' Sophie frowned.

'Daddy went over to her studio to see if you'd left a message for her. He said I wasn't to move out of the office.' Harry giggled, 'but it was boring in there and dark. Then I saw you through the window and I knew he wouldn't mind if I was with you.' He clung onto Sophie's arm. 'You're not leaving are you?' he demanded, picking up on her anxious look over her shoulder.

If Jack were in Emma's studio, it

wouldn't take him five minutes to check on her answerphone.

'I can't stay.'

'But you must,' Harry insisted. 'I want you and Daddy to be friends again then you and Bryony can come and live with us, can't you?'

'No, Harry, I can't. Your Daddy's engaged to Emma. She's going to be your new mother.'

'She isn't.' There was a mutinous jut to Harry's jaw as he argued with her. If the situation hadn't been so serious, Sophie would have laughed at his expression. It was a miniature reflection of his father's when something hadn't pleased him. 'Emma doesn't eat chocolate cake or chips and she says dog hairs are a nuisance 'cos they leave a mess on her sofa.'

'I'm sure they do,' Sophie agreed in an attempt to calm Harry down. She didn't want the child creating a scene and attracting Jack's attention. She tugged at her T shirt. 'Let me go, there's a good boy.'

'If I do, you won't come back,' Harry said with remarkable perspicacity for a child of such tender years. 'Will you?'

Sophie knew that to break a promise to a child was unforgivable.

'There's no need for me to come back,' she said softly.

'Yes there is. You've got to come back to see Daddy.'

'I don't think so. He's going to build a new life with Emma. They're going to get married.'

'No they aren't.'

'Your father is engaged to Emma.'

'No, I'm not.'

'Daddy.'

Harry swung round on Sophie's bag as he greeted his father. The action caused her to topple into Jack's arms. She crashed against the hard wall of his chest. Through her T shirt she could feel his heart beating a fast tattoo against hers.

'I know you said I was to stay in the office,' Harry raced through his explanation, 'but I saw Sophie outside, so I couldn't let her go before she'd seen you could I?'

'You did very well, Harry,' Jack smiled down at his son. 'Thank you.'

'I knew you'd be pleased. Can I have a doughnut?'

Sophie tried to wriggle out of Jack's hold, but his arms were stronger than a steel band around her waist and didn't budge.

'Let me go,' she hissed.

'Harry says I'm not allowed to,' he insisted with an infuriating smile, 'and I've discovered that if I want a quiet life it's best to do what my son tells me.'

'Don't be ridiculous.'

'Hello, you,' he said softly, into her hair.

'Stop it,' Sophie pleaded, aware her precarious hold on her self control was in danger of breaking down.

'When you're angry your nose goes all pink. Did you know that? Are you angry with me?'

'Why should I be angry with you?' Sophie tried to affect a casual reply.

'What you do is of absolutely no interest to me.'

'I think you're fibbing. You're miffed because of Emma. Admit it, you are, aren't you?'

'No.'

'Does that mean you're jealous?'

Sophie now felt the stirrings of real anger rise in her chest.

'I'm not jealous. I'm speechless. How can you be so disloyal to Emma? I suppose it gets easier the second time round. Once you've let one girl down practice makes perfect and you've got quite a track record.'

'That doesn't sound like speechless to me. How's Mary by the way?'

'She's fine. Don't change the subject.'

'My foot's recovering nicely too, thank you for asking.'

'If I wasn't such a lady, I'm so mad I'd kick it.'

'There really is no need to look at me like that. I told you I'm not engaged to Emma. You're the only girl for me.'

'What do you mean, you're not engaged to Emma?' Sophie demanded.

'Exactly what I said. We're not engaged. We never were.'

'So what's with the picture in the Gazette and the antique engagement ring? I didn't imagine the intimate supper in the Vista Lounge, did I? Will you stop smiling at me like that?'

'It's the only way I know how to smile and why didn't you answer my calls?'

'Why do you think?' she demanded.

'I don't know. Why don't you enlighten me?'

'Because I have no wish to have anything to do with a two timing womaniser.'

'Daddy,' Harry's voice bordered on a whimper. 'Are you and Sophie arguing again?'

'No, Harry, of course we're not,' Jack's voice was gentle as he replied to his son. 'Grown ups often talk like this to each other when they're in love.'

Sophie's cheeks flamed. 'I am not in love with you.'

'Does that mean you'll get married?'

Harry asked hopefully. 'Then I'd have a dog, wouldn't I?'

'I apologise for my son's one track mind,' Jack said. 'He's as bad as his father when he sets his mind on something. Harry wants a dog and I,' Jack paused then added in a voice that threatened to set fire to Sophie's fingertips, 'want you.'

'We could have chips for tea every day,' Harry crowed.

'What girl could refuse a proposal like that?'

'This one,' Sophie insisted. 'Now will you let go? I've a busy day ahead of me.'

As she struggled her envelope fluttered to the ground. Harry pounced on it.

'What's this?'

'It's for Emma, darling.' Sophie tried to take it from him but Jack wouldn't let go of her arms.

'She's not there,' Jack replied, adding, 'you can call me darling too if you like. I don't mind. Actually I'd find it rather nice.'

Sophie's head began to swim. 'Please,' she begged, 'let me go.'

'Why?'

'Because I have to see Emma.'

'She's not there. She's away.'

'Then I'll leave a message for her.'

'It could be a while before she reads it. She's on her honeymoon.'

Sophie blinked at Jack in confusion, suddenly grateful that his arms were still supporting her.

'What did you say?' she asked.

'Emma is away on honeymoon,' he repeated slowly.

'She's married Iain,' Harry put in helpfully. 'That's why she can't marry Daddy. I tried to tell her, Daddy,' Harry insisted, 'but she wouldn't listen to me.'

'I know the feeling,' Jack replied with a wry smile. 'She doesn't listen to me either. Would you like to sit down?' he asked as Sophie swayed against him.

'I'll get you a chair,' Harry offered and tore off in the direction of the office.

Sophie frowned at Jack. His eyes

were bloodshot and he didn't look as though he'd had much sleep recently.

'I've missed you.' His voice was a hoarse croak. 'You've no idea how much. Why didn't you answer my wretched telephone calls?'

'Because I have nothing to say to you.'

'I've plenty I want to say to you.'

'Here.'

There was a scraping noise as Harry dragged a wooden chair over the cobblestones.

'You can sit on this, Sophie. I'm sorry it's got paint on it. I was drawing you another picture of Bryony and my pot fell over. I tried to rub it off with my hankie. It's ever so red, isn't it?'

Harry looked up at her. His face threatened to crumple as he realised the enormity of his deed.

In the office the telephone began ringing. Jack didn't move. Neither did Harry

'Someone should answer it,' Sophie insisted.

'I'm not moving until you give Harry

and me an answer.'

'Come on, West, put that woman down.' His neighbour from unit 7A called across with a cheery wave in their direction. 'You don't want to have anything to do with him, love. He's already spoken for. I've seen him chatting up that Emma Mountjoy. Now, if you're looking for a real man, I'm available.'

'We can't talk here.' Jack raised his eyebrows in annoyance as the man strolled past.

'Daddy,' Harry piped up. 'I'm hungry.'

A fat blob of rain landed on the garage forecourt, another, then another swiftly followed it.

'For heaven's sake, not now,' Jack groaned. He tried to blink the moisture out of his eyes.

A bubble of laughter rose in Sophie's throat.

'What's so funny?' he demanded, shaking raindrops off his hair.

'You look like a shaggy dog,' Sophie said.

'The rain has washed the paint off

Daddy's chair. You can sit down now if you like, Sophie,' Harry said.

'Do you want to sit down?' Jack enquired.

'I'm getting wet,' Harry complained and tugged at Sophie's T shirt. 'Can we go inside?'

The last of Sophie's resistance crumbled. She had no idea what was going on, but with Emma safely married to Iain, she and Jack had no further claims on each other.

'Come on.' She finally managed to slip out of Jack's grasp. 'You'd better get that classic car under cover or you'll have an irate owner after you.'

'Where are you going?' Jack demanded.

'To shove this,' she held up her damp envelope, 'through Emma's letterbox before it gets ruined.'

Sophie no longer cared if Emma read the contents or not. She had done her job, and right now she had other priorities.

'Then what say I take Harry home with me for the rest of the day while you work on that car?'

'Yippee.' Harry did a little dance on the forecourt. 'Chips for lunch.'

'What about this evening?' Jack lowered his voice. His breath misted the air as he murmured in her ear, 'I have to talk to you privately without any interruptions.'

He semaphored with his eyes in Harry's direction.

'I suppose I could get my mother to give Harry a bed for the night if you like. She's used to small boys, she's got three grandsons. My parents will look after Bryony too if I ask them.'

'Are you sure your mother won't mind?'

'She'll be positively ecstatic if she thinks there's a man on the horizon. She's been trying to fix me up for years with her friends' sons.'

'I'm glad you resisted her persuasion. Dinner? Eight o'clock?'

'Anywhere but the golf club?'

'Check.' Jack smiled as the sun tried to break through the rain.

'Look, Daddy.' Harry splashed through an oily puddle as he jumped up and down and pointed towards the sky. 'A rainbow. Isn't it lovely? That's a sign of good things to come, isn't it?'

'I Couldn't Really Turn Her Down'

Jack carried the foil containers out onto the terrace on a tray. 'This is the second time I've done this to you, isn't it?' he apologised. 'It's a step up from baked beans on toast, but it's hardly a romantic dinner à deux is it?'

'It's lovely.' Sophie looked round the floodlit terrace. 'There's nowhere else I'd rather be,' she assured him. 'I love it here.'

'I got seriously held up at the garage because of the storm, then a difficult customer kept me hanging around while he decided exactly what he wanted doing to his car. I was on the point of telling him to remove his car from my premises by the time he'd made up his mind. Then when I tried to make a dinner reservation,' he gave a shamefaced smile, 'the only place who could take us for tonight was the golf club, so I passed on that one.'

'I don't think I ever want to go to their restaurant again,' Sophie said as she lifted the lid on a dish of fragrant lemon spiced rice.

'Understood.'

For a few moments they occupied themselves with the Thai dishes Jack had ordered from the takeaway. They were both drinking mint tea and Sophie knew the smell would always remind her of this night for the rest of her life.

The dark circles had disappeared from under Jack's eyes although his smile was still tired. Sophie experienced a fleeting pang of guilt. Between them they had wasted so much time.

'Who's going first?' Jack asked waving a tiger prawn in the air.

'You were the one who left all those urgent messages on my answering machine,' Sophie smiled, 'so I'll let you have that privilege.'

'It's difficult to know where to start.'

'I had this same conversation yesterday with Adam Baxter.'

Jack raised his eyebrows. 'The Adam Baxter as in the one there's been all the fuss about?'

'The very same.'

'And he came to see you?'

Sophie nodded. 'He lives in Spain now and calls himself Adam Garcia, but never mind all that. You owe me an explanation. Start with your engagement to Emma.'

'There was no engagement,' Jack replied. 'I know the Gazette did a feature on us but that was all part of the plan.'

'What plan?'

'It was a smokescreen, to put everyone off the scent.'

'You're going to have to talk me through this one slowly,' Sophie insisted, 'there have been enough misunderstandings between us already.'

'Emma and Iain only pretended to break up.'

'Why?'

'To get everyone off their backs.

That's why Emma wasn't taking any calls. She didn't want to talk to you because she didn't think she could convincingly pull the wool over your eyes and she thought you'd see through her story in a nanosecond.'

'The crafty old thing,' Sophie cut in.

'That reporter who broke the story about Emma's so called involvement with the Baxters provided Emma and Iain with a wonderful excuse to pretend to finish their relationship.'

'Only they didn't?'

'That's right. Even I didn't realise they were still together until Emma came round one evening and asked me for a big favour. When she told me what it was, I was reluctant to get involved but I couldn't really turn her down. She was there for me when my world fell apart and, well it was pay back time. You do understand, don't you?' The anxious look was back in Jack's eyes.

'Yes, of course,' Sophie replied in a soft voice, at the same time wishing Jack hadn't been so loyal to their old friend, 'I only wish you'd taken me into your confidence earlier.'

'I wanted to tell you what was happening, but I was sworn to secrecy then the news broke before I had the chance to say anything. I couldn't believe it when I read the story in the newspaper. The next thing I knew you weren't taking my calls and Emma had eloped and married in secret. I couldn't get over to visit you because my mother was in Canada and there was no-one to look after Harry. Life doesn't get a lot worse than that I can tell you.'

'But why did you tell me you weren't sure about your feelings for Emma and that you thought you might be in love with her?' Sophie asked as she sipped her tea to quench the dryness in her mouth.

'I was being economical with the truth,' Jack admitted. 'It's not something I make a habit of and I'm sorry, Sophie. You didn't deserve that sort of treatment, but,' he paused, 'I didn't think I would fall in love again. I didn't think it was possible. So every time I saw you I invented excuses not to like you. I couldn't believe someone as beautiful as you could be so perfect.'

Sophie was glad the light was fading from the day. It helped to disguise her blushes.

'I was sure it wasn't you who sold Emma's story to the press,' Jack ploughed on with his explanation, 'but I tried to convince myself it was. I should have followed my son's example,' Jack said.

'And run away with my dog?' Sophie quipped back at him, still trying to come to terms with what Jack was saying.

'He fell in love with you the first time he met you. Actually, I think his ardour might have had something to do with Bryony, but whatever, you seemed to have pressed the right button from the off. The few relationships I have had since I've been a single parent have always come to grief because of Harry. He has very high standards,' Jack confided with a smile.

'Chips and chocolate cake?' Sophie teased.

'Exactly, and a dog of course.'

'Of course,' Sophie agreed mock seriously.

'And you ticked all the boxes.'

'I'm glad I got something right.'

'We've a lot to be grateful to Harry for. Did you know one of the reasons he made off with Bryony that day in the market was an attempt to get us together? He confessed everything to my mother at bedtime. She's looking forward to meeting you by the way.'

'You've told her about me?' Sophie felt a qualm of concern. Goodness knows what the poor woman would make of her if Jack had delivered his honest opinion and Harry had banged on about a female who fed him chips and chocolate cake and let him run away with her dog.

'Harry has. I filled in the gaps. There's no need to look so worried. You got a good press,' Jack smile. 'So, there you have it. Now it's your turn,' he urged Sophie.

'There's not much to tell. You know most of my story. I can't tell you exactly why I was working for Emma because it would be a breach of client confidentiality.'

'Was it anything to do with Roger Mountjoy's marriage to Naomi Baxter?'

'You knew?' Sophie gaped at Jack in startled surprise. 'How? Why didn't you say anything earlier?'

'I didn't know that was the reason Emma employed you and I couldn't bring myself to read all the sordid details in the newspaper. I had better things to do, like running a garage.'

'But if you knew about Naomi, why didn't Emma know Naomi Baxter worked in her uncle's garage as his bookkeeper?'

'She hardly ever visited when I was there. She was away at school most of the time.'

Sophie nodded. That made sense. Emma was the least mechanically minded person in the world.

'I only really got to know her properly after she left school and when

I started dating Linda.'

'Right, well Emma thought it was possible that her father and Naomi Baxter were somehow involved.'

'You don't have to tell me this.'

'I can't see the harm now it appears to be public knowledge. Emma asked me to look into the matter because she didn't want any scandal coming to light after her engagement to Iain was announced. Then when she received an anonymous telephone call informing her that the story was about to break anyway, she asked me to stop my investigation.'

'Ah, yes. The anonymous telephone call.'

Sophie frowned. 'I never did find out who made it.'

'That was Iain's agent.'

'Sorry?'

'The anonymous telephone caller, she's a very formidable lady. Emma told me she doesn't let the grass grow under her feet. She works on the basis that there's no such thing as bad publicity so she nudged things along. Somehow or other she found out about Emma's involvement with you. I think she also tipped off those reporters about the two of you being in the wine bar that evening. That's why they were waiting outside for you.'

'Is there anything you don't know about this affair?' Sophie asked.

'I wasn't aware I knew anything at all,' Jack insisted.

'How did you find out about Naomi and Roger's marriage?'

'Roger asked me to look after the garage one Saturday morning while he and Naomi slipped out. I was in seventh heaven. I'd never been left in charge before so I didn't really pay much attention to what was going on. When they came back Roger told me they were married and that I wasn't to tell anyone. To be honest I forgot all about it. Teenage boys don't go much on marriage.'

'What about when she disappeared?'

'I missed that one too. Sorry,' Jack

apologised. 'Adolescence,' he added by way of explanation.

'No, thank you,' Sophie said as he offered her the last of the prawns.

He scooped them onto his plate. 'I didn't have any lunch,' he explained as he tucked in.

Sophie leaned back in her chair and listened to the night sounds coming from the water. The last time she had visited Riverside Cottage the evening had ended disastrously. She didn't want to go down that route again.

'Do you have any other issues?' she asked as Jack finished his prawns.

'Issues?' he frowned screwing up his paper napkin.

'We don't have problems these days,' Sophie explained. 'We have issues to be resolved.'

'We've had a fair amount of those,' Jack admitted with his slow smile. 'But,' he held up his hand and ticked them off on his fingers. 'I've apologised for behaving like a boor?'

Sophie pretended to consider the

question then relented as a look of alarm spread across Jack's face.

'Go on,' she urged. 'What's the next issue?'

'I never for a moment thought you'd be so cheap as to sell Emma's story to the newspapers.'

'I believe you.'

'And there really is nothing of a romantic nature between Emma and me.'

'I should hope not if she really is married to Iain.'

'She is. They're on their honeymoon. Is that it?' Jack asked.

Now the moment had come, Sophie didn't know how to deal with it.

'I'm not very good with words,' Jack admitted. 'Every time I open my mouth I seem to get in a mess.' He leaned across the rickety garden table, 'but I really do mean what I say this time, Sophie.'

She raised her eyes to his.

'Go on,' she urged quietly, unwilling to break the spell between them.

'If you could put up with an old man

of thirty-six and face the challenge of being an instant mother to a five-year-old and if I promise never to accuse you of being an undercover reporter again, would you do me the very great honour of being my wife?'

'I come with baggage too. What about my work?'

'I have no issues with that,' Jack smiled.

'And Bryony?' Sophie reminded him gently. 'She'll have to be part of the family unit and you've always said Harry couldn't have a dog.'

'We'll sort something out.'

He drew Sophie to her feet. For the second time that day she felt Jack's heartbeat against hers. It was steady as a drum.

'Not good enough,' Sophie insisted. 'I don't want Bryony feeling left out.'

'Why don't we give her to Harry as a wedding present?' Jack suggested.

Sophie raised her face to his.

'Well? You haven't answered my question,' he said, his eyes searching hers.

'I think that's a very good idea.'

'About getting married?'

'About giving Bryony to Harry.'

'You know what I mean.' Jack's voice was almost a growl.

'Will you break the news to Harry or shall I?'

'Will you marry me?' His voice startled a snoozing duck.

'There's no need to shout,' Sophie said, 'and before we have another misunderstanding, the answer's yes.'

She was no longer aware of the night noises from the river, the quacking ducks or the fact that they were standing in the middle of a spotlight in full view of passers by walking the towpath. Jack's lips descending on hers drove all other considerations from her mind.

As they finally drew apart, Sophie smiled.

'Emma was right,' she said.

'What was that?' Jack asked.

'I'm seeing stars,' she replied. 'Kiss me again.'

We do hope that you have enjoyed reading this large print book.

Did you know that all of our titles are available for purchase?

We publish a wide range of high quality large print books including:
Romances, Mysteries, Classics
General Fiction
Non Fiction and Westerns

Special interest titles available in large print are:
The Little Oxford Dictionary
Music Book, Song Book
Hymn Book, Service Book

Also available from us courtesy of Oxford University Press:
Young Readers' Dictionary
(large print edition)
Young Readers' Thesaurus
(large print edition)

For further information or a free brochure, please contact us at:
Ulverscroft Large Print Books Ltd.,
The Green, Bradgate Road, Anstey,
Leicester, LE7 7FU, England.
Tel: (00 44) **0116 236 4325**
Fax: (00 44) **0116 234 0205**

SECRETS IN THE SAND

Jane Retallick

When Sarah Daniels moves to a sleepy Cornish village her neighbour, local handyman and champion surfer, Ben Trelawny is intrigued. He falls in love with her stunning looks and quirky ways — but who is this woman? Why does she lock herself in her cottage — and why she is so guarded? When Ben finally gets past Sarah's barriers, a national newspaper reporter arrives in the village. Sarah disappears, making a decision that puts her life and future in jeopardy.

WITHOUT A SHADOW OF DOUBT

Teresa Ashby

Margaret Harris's boss, Jack Stanton, disappears in suspicious circumstances. The police want to track him down, but Margaret believes in him and wants to help him prove his innocence. Meanwhile, Bill Colbourne wants to marry her, but, unsure of her feelings, she can't think of the future until she finds Jack. And, when she does meet with him in Spain, she finally has to admit to Bill that she can't marry him — it's Jack Stanton who she loves.